S0-AJM-190

The Girl with Spunk

The Girl with Spunk

by JUDITH ST. GEORGE

Illustrated by Charles Robinson

Cover by Leonard Shortall

SCHOLASTIC BOOK SERVICES

NEW YORK • TORONTO • LONDON • AUCKLAND • SYDNEY • TOKYO

To Peter

No part of this publication may be reproduced in whole or in part, or stored in a retrieval system, or transmitted in any form or by any means, electronic, mechanical, photocopying, recording, or otherwise, without written permission of the publisher. For information regarding permission, write to Scholastic Book Services, 50 West 44th Street, New York, NY 10036.

Copyright © 1975 by Judith St. George. This edition is published by Scholastic Book Services, a division of Scholastic Magazines, Inc., by arrangement with G. P. Putnam's Sons.

12 11 10 9 8 7 6 5 4 3 2 1   1   7 8 9/7 0 1 2/8

Contents

The Homecoming

Josie knelt down beside the open hayloft windows, sinking deep into the prickly hay. She couldn't see out the windows, but she knew her uncle on the ground below couldn't see her either.

"Josie Dexter, I know you're hiding in that barn, and I'm going to stand here till you come down!" Josie heard her Uncle Hiram shout. She could picture him, tall and powerful, with dark side-whiskers that reached almost to the corners of his mouth. From the sound of his voice, Josie guessed he was standing by the corner of the barn.

She would just have to stay where she was. She was safe up in the hayloft, and they both knew it. Uncle Hiram had a stiff leg and couldn't climb up the loft ladder after her.

Josie flopped over in the hay, upset at how the evening had turned out. She worked as a hired girl in town, and it was hard to get time to see her family. But tonight she had finished her work early. Figuring her uncle would be out

1

shooting woodchucks after supper as usual, she walked out to the farm for a visit with her mother and her brothers. She had made a birthday dress and bonnet for her mother and brought them with her.

But Uncle Hiram had surprised her by being home, and she had clambered into the loft to escape his anger. Josie had spent part of her wages on her mother's dress goods and real glass buttons. Her uncle was furious. All of Josie's wages belonged to him!

Josie carefully placed the basket that held the dress and bonnet beside her and lay down in the hay. It still smelled of the sun and warmth of the fields as if it had just been brought in fresh that day. Even though haying was backbreaking work, Josie missed the farm in summertime, when the hot sun baked out the moist hay and the crickets and katydids set up their evening din. Being hired help in town was as hard as farmwork, but without any of the country pleasures. She especially missed the birds, following a meadowlark to his nest or flushing out a convoy of quail as she walked through the meadow.

Josie clasped her hands behind her head and watched the barn swallows swoop in and out of the barn as they fed their young. But tonight she was too upset to enjoy the birds. Uncle Hiram was a stubborn man. He might wait out there all night. And Josie had to be back in town early in the morning.

Uncle Hiram had been her father's brother, and when Josie's father had died five years ago, the farm had gone to Hiram. Both brothers were tall, strong men, but Josie's father, John, had been a quiet man with laughing eyes. Hiram Dexter's eyes seldom laughed, and his face was lined with bitterness. Different as the two men had been, Josie's mother had married Hiram within a year.

"Josie Dexter, there's no way you can get outta that loft without me seeing you," she heard her uncle call out.

Josie sat bolt upright. This time she heard something in his voice she hadn't noticed before. His words were slurred. Not much, but enough for her to know he had been drinking. That's probably why he hadn't gone 'chuck hunting. Josie edged closer to the hayloft windows and looked out. She could see the vine-shaded well house and the farmhouse beyond it. The red clapboard of the house was chipped and peeling, not painted since her father died. Behind the house were her mother's gardens, with the hollyhocks and clove pinks and rows of herbs neatly tended, not run-down like the rest of the farm.

Uncle Hiram was just beyond the corner of the barn so Josie couldn't see him. Then, suddenly, he walked into view, followed by his hound, Toby. He was leaning on his walking stick and dragging his stiff left leg more than usual. That was all Josie had to see. The more Uncle Hiram drank, the more he limped. Now nothing would get her down there. Drinking made him ugly.

Josie backed away from the windows with a sigh. Since she was stuck, she might as well spend the last half hour of daylight reading. Right now, reading was the only thing that might get her mind off Uncle Hiram. Josie's book was packed in the bottom of the basket under her mother's new drss. She dug it out. *Ivanhoe* by Sir Walter Scott. A novel. Novels were her favorite books.

Without meaning to, her thoughts turned back to Hiram Dexter. He called novels worthless trash. He was as set against novels as he had been set against schooling. Two years ago, when Josie was twelve, he had made her quit school and go to work. He said educating a girl was a waste of his money, especially when she could be earning wages of her own. At least he hadn't signed her up at the local woolen mill, where the long hours were spent in airless lofts and the noise of the machinery was deafening. Josie had been hired out as a servant girl to the Brown family in town.

Josie opened her book to where she had left off, determined to forget Uncle Hiram. "The tramp of horses was now heard, and the Lady Rowena appeared, surrounded by several riders, and a much stronger party of footmen . . ." she read. By the end of two or three pages Josie had pushed thoughts of her uncle to the back of her mind. Instead of hiding in the hayloft of a shabby farm in Waterloo, New York, in the year 1848, she rode deep in the medieval forests of *Ivanhoe*.

The sun lowered, and the daylight dimmed. Josie stretched out near the windows to catch the last rays of the sun as they reddened and died. But the words on the page began to blur. The stirrings of the horses in their stalls and the cooing of the pigeons lulled her. Unlike the ladies of old, Josie had spent the day scrubbing down the Browns' kitchen and boiling tin tubs of wash, and she was tired. She closed the book and laid her head on her outstretched arm. She slept deeply.

"Sst, Josie." She was immediately awake.

It was her brother Sam's voice. Josie sat up. Night had fallen, but the full moon was so bright she could make out Sam's stocky body as he crawled through the hay toward her.

She reached for him. "What is it, Sam?"

"It's Uncle Hiram. You got to help," Sam whispered back, though there was no one to hear but a few fluttering swallows.

Josie dreaded what was coming. "Wh-wh-what about him?" she asked. When she was small, Josie had stuttered badly. Now she only did it when she was upset.

"He's drunk and real mean with Ma," Sam answered. In the moonlight, Josie could see how frightened he was.

Uncle Hiram must have started drinking in earnest. "I'll come," she said. She dreaded to think what her uncle would do when he saw her. But she had to help. Though Sam was tall and husky, as their father had been, he was only nine. Robert was twelve, but small for his age and slight.

Josie hiked up her skirts and half slid, half fell down the loft ladder. Sam scrambled down behind her. As they landed on the stone floor, the barn cats scattered in alarm. Josie led the way toward the house, the full moon lighting the path. A quick look at how far the Big Dipper had swung around the North Star, and

Josie knew it was very late. If Uncle Hiram had been drinking all night, he would be in a rage.

As Josie pushed open the backyard gate, she heard a crash and her uncle's cursing from inside. The kitchen door was ajar, just as Sam had left it. Josie ran in. Only a lard-oil lamp was burning, but the kitchen was bright with moonlight. Josie's mother was backed up against the fireplace with an iron fry pan in her hand. Robert, in his nightshirt, was by her side. Though Susan Dexter was small, she was strong. But she was afraid of her husband, and Josie knew her mother would never defend herself.

Hiram paced up and down the opposite side of the kitchen. A rye whiskey jug lay smashed against the fireplace. Toby made a fearful racket as he bounded across the kitchen, barking and howling.

"Are you all right, Ma?" Josie asked.

At the sound of her daughter's voice, Susan Dexter turned, and Josie saw the right side of her face was red and swollen. Uncle Hiram must have hit her!

"I'm all right, Josie," she answered, keeping her eye on her husband as a mouse would watch a circling cat.

Uncle Hiram whirled on Josie. "So you decided to show up, after all, did you? Don't figger I don't know what you're up to. You kept part of your wages for yourself, that's what. Robbers, all of you!" He started to pace again, up and down, his left leg thudding with each step. His speech was thick. "You're just like your ma, girl, hiding money from me, just the way she done." He waved his walking stick in his wife's direction.

"I earned that money sewing gloves, Hiram. I only used it to buy myself new tinware," Susan Dexter protested. But she sounded frightened.

"Who runs this farm and puts a roof over all your heads? I gave up everything I wanted for myself to come live here." Hiram's tanned face was flushed. "What would you have done after John died if I hadn't taken over?"

"We'd have done better, that's what. We-we-we'd have managed," Josie replied, surprising even herself. In the face of anger, she usually got quieter and quieter. But the red mark on her mother's face shocked her into speaking out.

"You . . . you. . . ." Uncle Hiram's deep-lined face seemed to swell with fury. He strode across the kitchen, raising his walking stick high over his head and bringing it down

toward Josie. She only had time to raise her arm to shield her face. The stick whacked down on her and a sharp pain ran up her arm. As she fell back under the blow, her heel caught in the edge of a braided rug. She slipped and crashed to the floor, striking the side of her head on the corner of the kitchen table. Dimly Josie heard her mother call out, but she couldn't see her. Even Toby's frantic barking faded into a swirling emptiness as everything went black around her.

An Apology

The sorrowful churr-churr of mourning doves awakened Josie before dawn. She lay quietly for a moment listening to their sad call. For a long time she had thought of the birds as "morning" doves. Then one day she had realized their melancholy cooing was a "mourning" song. It was the perfect name for them.

It was still dark, but the gray of the sky seemed to be lifting, so she guessed it was after four. The cool air of the past few days had turned humid and hot overnight, and her petticoat was twisted around her legs and damp from the heat. She threw back the sheeting and kicked her legs free from her skirts. She could still steal another half hour's sleep before starting the Browns' breakfast.

As Josie closed her eyes and rolled over, pain in her left arm startled her fully awake. She wasn't in her bed at the Browns' at all. She was home, in her old bedroom. Then the memory of what happened last night rushed back to her. Uncle Hiram had been drunk and hit her with his stick. No wonder her arm hurt. And she had fallen. Josie lifted her hand and gingerly felt her face. Sure enough, there was a lump as big as a partridge egg right beside her eye where she had struck the table. Her mother and the boys must have helped her up to bed.

Swinging her bare feet to the floor, Josie stood up. Her head felt a little wobbly, but no bones seemed to be broken. Though her arm hurt, she could move it. She poured some water from her bedside pitcher into the washbowl and rinsed her face. The water was soupy warm. It was going to be a hot day.

The sun was already clearing the last of the stars from the sky. It was more than time to start back to town. Mrs. Brown expected her to be on hand to fix breakfast as usual, no matter what. Quickly Josie dressed. As she bent over to button her shoes, the rays of the rising sun glinted off the looking glass that hung on the opposite wall. Almost afraid to see how she looked, Josie lifted the glass off its hook and carried it to the light of the window.

It was just as she had feared. The lump didn't show much, but her eye was turning color. Josie groaned. She knew it would look worse before it looked better. And the face that went with it wouldn't be the handsomer for a black eye. She studied her reflection. Broomstickstraight brown hair all snarled from not having been brushed from its knot last night. A sharp, thin face, with wide gray eyes set far apart and a narrow pointed nose that her pa had always said she got from poking into books so much.

From the barnyard, Josie heard the first crowing of Mr. Clay, the rooster. She had to smile. He always sounded as if he were practicing a little before he began, just like a singer. Josie hung the looking glass back on the wall and tidied up the bed, using her sore left arm as little as possible. Mrs. Brown had watermelon rinds soaking in salt water overnight for pickling, and there was all the ironing to do from yesterday's wash. Josie was anxious to get at the work before the heat of the day closed in. Tomorrow, Sunday, was her once-a-month free day, and if her chores weren't finished, she might not be able to take it.

There was a light tap on the door. "Josie?" a voice called softly.

It was Uncle Hiram. Josie couldn't see him. She wouldn't! She whirled around, but the loft room, with only space for the bed, a chair, and a chest of drawers, offered no hiding place. Then she thought of her mother. Suppose Uncle Hiram had harmed her after Josie had been put to bed last night. Maybe she needed help. Josie yanked open the door. Uncle Hiram stood in the dark of the hall, his face hidden in the shadows.

"Is Ma all right?"

Uncle Hiram nodded. "She's still asleep," he said in a hoarse voice. As he entered the room, Josie smelled the odor of stale whiskey. And when he stepped into the path of the sunlight, Josie could see he hadn't changed his clothes. More than likely, he hadn't been to bed at all. His hair was even more tangled than hers, and his sun-browned face looked blotchy.

"I brought you fresh water," Hiram said. He held out a china pitcher with shaky hands. "And I wanted to talk to you before you head back to Waterloo."

Josie took the cool pitcher and set it on the chest of drawers. "I've already washed," she said. She couldn't bring herself to meet his eyes.

"That was an accident last night, you knocking your head on that table and all. Still, I feel bad about it," Hiram said. His speech was slow.

"What about you hitting Ma?" Josie demanded. She was angry all over again at the thought. Never, never would Pa have done such a thing.

"It's the whiskey," Uncle Hiram mumbled. "It gets a-hold on me, and I ain't myself."

Then keep away from it, Josie wanted to shout. But she said nothing.

Hiram glanced at her with red and swollen eyes. It was as if he had heard her. "You know I try to stay off the whiskey, girl," he said. "But when I get to thinking what mighta been . . ." His words trailed off.

"I got to go," Josie said hastily. She stepped around him and left the room. Just as sure as owls prowled at night, Uncle Hiram got to feeling sorry for himself after one of his drunk spells. He blamed God, fate, the lockkeeper, the mules, and everybody but himself for how his barge broke up and smashed his leg before it sank in the Erie Canal. And Josie didn't want to hear it again and start to feel sorry for him herself. The trouble was, she did feel sorry for him. He had been happy on the canal, and farming came hard to him. But the memory of last night was too fresh for her sympathy this morning. She hurried down the loft stairs.

As Josie passed her mother and her uncle's bedroom, she looked in. Susan Dexter was awake, lying on her back in bed, staring out the window.

Josie was surprised her mother was still in bed. "I'm leaving now, Ma. Good-bye," she called.

At the sound of Josie's voice, her mother

turned toward her, raising herself on her elbows. She looked pale, and her face had a pinched expression. "Your eye is swelled up, Josie. Will your head be too sore to work today?" she asked.

Josie tried to smile. "It's fine, Ma. It looks worse than it feels."

"What happened last night ain't like Hiram. He didn't mean none of it at all," Susan Dexter said softly. "It's the hard life, never getting anywhere and the work never ceasing. All men got to turn to the whiskey sometimes. Hiram's a good husband and provides for me and the boys."

"I guess so," Josie murmured. But she remembered her father never had to turn to the whiskey, no matter how bad things got. "Goodbye, Ma. I'll try to get home again in a couple of weeks."

She gave her mother a quick wave and slipped out through the kitchen. Grabbing a handful of cold soda biscuits and two ripe peaches to eat on her way, Josie started toward the east pasture as a shortcut to town. She had better hurry. If breakfast wasn't ready right at seven, Mrs. Brown would be mad as a hornet.

As soon as Josie ran into the east pasture,

Blossom, one of the Dexters' cows, headed toward her. Blossom's brass bell clanged as she moaned to be milked. She was a grumbler, and all of a sudden, Josie smiled when she realized how much Blossom looked like Mrs. Brown complaining that Josie was late again.

"I'll have breakfast in jig time, Mrs. Brown," she called out.

The sight of the sad-looking cow gave Josie an idea. Old Mrs. Abbott's dairy farm was only a half mile or so beyond the Dexters', and she delivered milk in Waterloo every morning. Though Mrs. Abbott had always been peculiar from other farm folk, and with age was growing even more so, she would be making a delivery at the Browns' and maybe could give Josie a ride. If Josie hurried, she might still catch Mrs. Abbott before she started out for town.

"The Sow Got the Measles"

The early dew that winked on the grass and wild flowers soaked Josie's skirts as she headed for the woods that separated the two farms. Even on a bright day, the woods were dark, but with the sun barely up, they were still deep in shadows. But Josie didn't care. She knew the woods as well as the rooms in her own house. She could never guess how many hours she had spent in the woods studying and watching the birds. It was here she had first seen a pileated woodpecker. He had been whacking away at a tree with the strength of a man wielding an ax. She had never forgotten either the sight of the foot-and-a-half-long bird or the racket he made. Birds had fascinated Josie ever since that day.

As Josie ran from the gloom of the woods into the sunlight, she saw that Mrs. Abbott had already turned her cows out to pasture and backed her milk wagon up to the spring-house. "Hey there, Mrs. Abbott," Josie shouted as she saw the old lady swing the last barrel of

milk into her wagon and slam the tailgate shut. "Can you give me a ride to Waterloo?"

"Who goes there?" Mrs. Abbott called back. She squinted at Josie, her forehead pinched into a frown.

"Just me, Josie Dexter, looking for a ride into Waterloo," Josie answered as she reached the wagon. She gave Mrs. Abbott's horse, Rubin, a rub on the nose. "I go to work at the Browns' over to Williams Street, and I should be there by now." Though she had been working for the Browns the past two years, she was never sure what Mrs. Abbott remembered and what she didn't.

"Oh, Josephine, hop aboard." Mrs. Abbott grinned, climbing onto the narrow wagon bench and signaling for Josie to join her. As Josie swung herself up, Mrs. Abbott clucked at her horse. "Hurry it up there, girl. It's well past five, and Rubin's raring to go," she declared. "He knows folks want their milk early."

Rubin didn't look in a hurry to go anywhere, but Josie just smiled, and Mrs. Abbott smiled back. Lots of people thought of Mrs. Abbott as crazy. Maybe it was because her hair was white as a snowball bush and cut close all over her head, shorter even than a man's. Or maybe it was because she had a cackle of a laugh that burst out like a firecracker over what no one else thought was funny. She dipped snuff too, and not many people still did that, especially women. There was no doubt she was different and always did what she wanted, no matter what anyone thought. Because Josie had never quite made up her mind about Mrs. Abbott, she usually kept her distance.

Mrs. Abbott dropped the reins in her lap and clucked again as Rubin started through the gate and headed east toward town without any direction from her. The barrels of milk in the back of the wagon rattled and sloshed as they clattered over the bumpy road.

"So he's at it again," Mrs. Abbott said as if she and Josie had just been talking.

Bewildered, Josie tilted her head at Mrs. Abbott.

"Your eye, Josephine. What that Hiram Dexter did to your eye," she snapped as if Josie were an idiot not to know she had a black eye. "I know how Hiram drowns himself in sauce, then goes on a tear."

"It was nothing." Josie gulped. "I fell, that's all, and hit my head."

"You can't fool me, Josephine." Mrs. Abbott snorted. "I've known Hiram since the day he was born. Seen him change too. Funny thing, as a boy Hiram had a twinkle in his eye, and everyone liked him. I can recall when your pa and him was young, they used to play pranks on their ma that curled her hair with fright. But then life turned sour on Hiram. He become a different man."

Mrs. Abbott shook her head sadly. "The way Hiram is now, if he ain't willing to join the State Temperance Society and stay off the whiskey, your ma oughta leave him bag and baggage. That's what I did to my husband. I didn't so much leave him, 'course, as toss him out. The no-good. Died of the drink a year later. With him gone, running the dairy on my own's been hard work, 'specially now my rheumatism has got so bad. And my back ain't strong enough to lift them barrels anymore. I'd hire a strapping girl like you if I could afford it. Still, I'm proud of what I done on my own." Mrs. Abbott let out with one of her wild laughs that sent a shiver down Josie's back.

She edged over on the seat as Mrs. Abbott leaned toward her and tapped her on the knee with a snuff-stained finger. "Now your ma's smart about some things, but she got no sense about Hiram. She's ascairt of him, and he knows it. He's beat up on her more'n she'd ever let on, I can tell you."

At the mention of her mother, Josie suddenly remembered the dress she had left in the barn loft. All that work. Sewing came so hard for her. She'd had to rip out some seams three times before she had been satisfied. How would her mother ever know the dress was up there? Maybe the boys would find it before mice or squirrels chewed into the basket. But that was too risky. She turned to Mrs. Abbott.

"I made Ma a new dress and bonnet and left them in our hayloft. Could you let Ma know they're up there, Mrs. Abbott?" she asked. "I brought them out from town last night so's Ma could wear them on the morrow for church."

" 'Course I will, Josephine," Mrs. Abbott agreed. "I'll go straight away when I get back from Waterloo. I'd aimed to ask her to go to Seneca Falls with me anyways. . . ."

Josie hardly listened to the rest. As soon as she knew the dress would be safe, her thoughts turned to her own plans for the morrow. On her free day off from the Browns' she had planned to take a steamboat ride up Seneca Lake. She had even persuaded Mr. Brown to let her keep part of her wages for the fare. But then she had remembered her mother's birthday and spent it all on the dress goods. Well, she would have to go up the lake some other time. It would be nice just to have the day to herself.

" 'Twouldn't hurt you to go as well as your ma," Mrs. Abbott said as she took a box of clove-scented snuff from her apron pocket and dipped her black gum twig into it. She rubbed the snuff over her teeth and gums, then stuck the twig in the corner of her mouth sucking noisily on it. "I can't fancy women running the meeting, but no men are invited for the first day. That would be something to behold now, wouldn't it?" Mrs. Abbott chuckled.

Josie hadn't been listening, figuring only a nod or murmur of agreement was needed, so the old woman's words caught her up short. "What meeting?" she asked.

Mrs. Abbott turned to glare at Josie, her faded blue eyes sharp. "You got blinders on your ears like Rubin's blinders on his eyes, girl," she cracked. "I'm talking about the meeting that was announced in Thursday's newspaper. Didn't you read it? There's a ladies' convention next week over to Seneca Falls to discuss what rights women oughta have, but don't."

"Like what?" Josie asked.

"Like the right of a woman to hold onto her own property, that's what," Mrs. Abbott retorted. "Such as your ma. When your pa died without leaving a will, 'stead of ending up with only a third of the farm, she shoulda gotten all of it. Hiram getting two-thirds mighta been legal, but it weren't right."

Josie was suddenly interested. "That's true enough. But what can be done about it?"

"Try to get the laws changed, that's what. Write to the legislature. Petition. Protest," Mrs. Abbott said.

"What good would my protest be?" Josie asked.

"You'll never know if you don't try," Mrs. Abbott snapped. "Write to the state government in Albany. Speak up at meetings. Be heard."

Everyone wanted to be heard. Who wanted to listen? No one, that's who. Talk never got anything done. Mrs. Abbott's advice wasn't any better than anyone else's. Josie's attention wandered as her ears picked up the warbling song of a rose-breasted grosbeak. The grosbeak was lovely to hear, but hard to spot. She scanned the treetops that lined the road, but couldn't see him anywhere.

How do you think I began in this world?
I got me a sow and sev'ral other things.

Sow or hog or some such thing,
The sow got the measles and she died in
    the spring.

Mrs. Abbott sang out at the top of her lungs in a screeching soprano that made Josie forget all about the grosbeak.

"Mrs. Abbott," she gasped. They were on the outskirts of Waterloo, just passing the town pasture. Two women milking their cows turned to stare. It didn't seem to bother Mrs. Abbott. She swung into the second verse:

What do you think I made of her hide?
The very best saddle you ever did ride.
Saddle or bridle or some such thing,
The sow got the measles and she died in
    the spring.

She sang on, waving her snuff twig in time to the music.

"Oh, please, Mrs. Abbott," Josie pleaded. A farm wagon going in the opposite direction slowed down. The driver laughed out loud and tipped his broad-brimmed hat. Mrs. Abbott finished the second verse in the same piercing soprano and started on the third.

What do you think I made of her feet?
The very best pickles you ever did eat.

Pickles or glue or some such thing,
The sow got the measles and she died in
  the spring.

Even Rubin shook his head as if to clear his ears, and a dog sitting on the front steps of Waterloo House joined in with a long howl.

"Everyone's looking at us," Josie pointed out, praying that Mrs. Abbott would stop. But she finished to the very end.

"Let 'em look. You need stirring up, missy, or you'd dream your life away," Mrs. Abbott said, slapping Josie's knee again. "I got important news to tell you, and you're building air castles a million miles away. You're like a nice bowl of bread dough, Josephine. You got all the right ingredients, but they need punching and kneading and fire from an oven to make 'em into a worthwhile loaf of bread," she said. She settled her snuff twig back in her mouth.

"Anyways, now that my singing got your attention, maybe you'll listen," Mrs. Abbott continued. "When you get to the Browns', you hunt out a copy of Thursday's newspaper and read up on that woman's rights meeting. And you plan on going to it, hear?"

"Oh, yes, ma'am, I sure do hear," Josie replied hastily. Everybody was right. Mrs.

Abbot was crazy, and as soon as they reached the Browns', Josie would measure out their two pitchers of milk, thank Mrs. Abbott politely for the ride, and next time make sure she had some other way to get into town.

The Black Eye

Mrs. Brown was already in the kitchen when Josie ran in the back door. "Morning, Josie, you're late. And after I asked you to be here on time. Shame," she clucked as Josie picked up two tin pitchers to measure their day's supply of milk from Mrs. Abbott.

When she returned with the brimming jugs, Mrs. Brown was still talking, more to herself than to Josie. "Well, I guess it doesn't matter so long as Mr. Brown gets fed on time," she said, scooping out cornmeal for the griddle cakes. "Goodness, it's going to be a hot day, and what a night I had." She sighed. "I didn't sleep a wink, what with the heat and a cat howling outside my window and Mr. Brown's snoring and tossing all night."

Like Toby, Mrs. Brown's bark was worse than her bite, and Josie didn't pay much attention to her complaining. Despite her mutterings, Mrs. Brown treated her decently and never asked Josie to do more than was reasonable. She was a huge woman, both broad and tall, with a perpetually breathless air as if her whalebone corset were laced too tight.

Mr. Brown was heavy too, but more cheerful than his wife, and pleasanter. Though Mrs. Brown smiled a lot, her smile never reached her eyes. Mr. Brown didn't smile much, but Josie had long ago caught onto his act. Mr. Brown was an officer at the Seneca County Bank and had a reputation to uphold. Waterloo was a growing village with close to three thousand people. Businesses had sprung up. A railroad ran through town, and mills and factories, powered by the Seneca River and the Seneca and Cayuga Canal, flourished. Mr. Brown had become a man of importance in Waterloo, and Josie had decided he appeared stern and forbidding just to hide his soft heart.

"It's too hot to bake beans all day, but Saturday wouldn't be Saturday without them. As for the ironing, Josie, you can set up the board by the door and try to catch a breeze. . . ." Mrs. Brown always listed the day's chores as she and Josie prepared breakfast. The Browns' routine never varied from month to month, and after two years with the family, Josie was able to listen with half an ear. If Mrs. Brown wanted anything out of the ordinary, a second sense warned Josie to listen. Otherwise, her day was predictable.

First she had to get the stove going. She opened the door under the grate and cleaned out the ashes from the night before, then threw in some kindling chips. As soon as she had a good fire started, she filled the stove from the woodbox. Coffee was next. Mr. Brown liked his coffee hot and strong and on the table when he sat down. Fry the ham, and toss in the sausages. Mrs. Brown started the griddle cakes while the coffee boiled.

Since her work took no real thought, Josie planned what she would do on the morrow, her free day. She might hike to Montezuma Swamp to hunt for the great blue herons reported to be nesting there. Or maybe look for Indian relics near Old Black Brook. Or just go fishing. As Josie turned the sausages in the pan, she realized Mrs. Brown had stopped talking and was looking at her indignantly.

"Josie, don't you ever listen?" she asked in an exasperated voice.

"I'm sorry, Mrs. Brown. I-I . . . was thinking on something else," Josie apologized.

"I asked what happened to your eye." Mrs. Brown reached out and took Josie by the chin, turning her face to the light.

"I tripped on a rug last night and hit my head on a table," Josie explained. She wanted to pull away from Mrs. Brown's firm grasp but didn't dare. After all, her black eye wasn't Mrs. Brown's concern. Still, in a village like Waterloo, everyone expected to know everyone else's business.

"Tripped? That doesn't sound like you, Josie." Mrs. Brown looked thoughtful. She dropped her hand from Josie's face. "Are you sure you're all right?"

"Oh, yes, Mrs. Brown. It hardly hurts at all," Josie assured her.

"There wasn't trouble at the farm, was there?" Mrs. Brown asked.

"I fell, that's all," Josie insisted.

Fortunately, at that moment, Mrs. Brown and Josie heard Mr. Brown's footsteps come down the stairs and head toward the dining room. Will Brown came bounding down on his father's heels, and the black eye was forgotten.

"You're back, Josie, you're back," Will called as the kitchen door flew open, and his chunky little body hit Josie square on, his arms wrapping around her legs. Will Brown, seven years old and as chubby as his parents, had attached himself to Josie from the day she had arrived, and the affection was mutual.

"I had another nightmare last night, Josie,"

he bragged. "A bad one, with a giant crocodile that chased me right up Main Street. He was just like that one we saw on the canalboat last month."

Josie stooped down and straightened his collar. Will's square face and wide eyes reminded her of her brother Sam. "You only had a nightmare because you counted on having one," she said solemnly. "I promised I'd be back this morning, and here I am."

"I couldn't be sure, Josie," Will answered, putting his hands on her shoulders. "And that was a scary crocodile we saw. Remember the man said he could swallow a boy like me in one bite?"

"Fine thing. You've been in the kitchen five minutes and haven't even said good morning to your own mother." Though Mrs. Brown's voice was tart, her gap-toothed smile seemed to stretch from ear to ear. Wiping her wet hands on her apron, she picked up her son for a hug. But he wiggled out of her arms, grabbed a handful of sugar cookies from the tin, and ran from the kitchen. He slammed the door behind him.

Mrs. Brown shook her head, and the false curls by her ears bounced. "Imagine me with a married daughter and two grandchildren trying to raise that seven-year-old tornado." She laughed when she said it, and so did Josie. Will was a roly-poly imp, and though he was usually a sunny child, lately he had been troubled by nightmares that only Josie seemed able to comfort. If anyone had asked her opinion, she would have said he ate too much. But no one asked her, and Will continued to stuff himself.

"Rhoda, come join me for breakfast," the two women heard Mr. Brown call from the dining room, and they hurried. Mrs. Brown stacked the hot griddle cakes on a platter, then untied her apron, so she could sit with her husband and be served like a lady, just as if she hadn't been working since five o'clock.

By midmorning Josie's skirts hung on her hot and heavy as a blanket. The watermelon pickles were boiling on the stove, and the Boston beans and rye-and-injun bread were baking in the oven. Though all the windows were open, the kitchen was steamy hot, and thick with the smell of cooking food. Josie's head, which had been aching for an hour, began to throb. She picked up a clean dishcloth and slipped out the back door. It took only a moment to lower the bucket deep into the back-porch well and raise a brimming pailful of clear water. She splashed her arms and face and felt the iron band around her head loosen.

No one was about. Mrs. Brown had gone marketing, and Will had carried his pet rabbit next door to play with a friend. The Browns' two pigs were asleep in the mud of the shaded pigpen, and the chickens were indifferently pecking for feed by the carriage house. Josie sat down under the shadow of the cherry tree and pulled her skirts above her knees. When she laid the wet dishcloth over her eyes, the terrible pounding in her head began to ease.

"Josie Dexter, you're a sight," she heard a voice giggle. "And with Mr. Brown and all his friends arriving at the front door this very minute for their noonday dinner."

Josie snatched the cloth from her head and yanked down her skirts. "Mr. Brown, where?" she cried. Then she fell back against the tree. "Oh, Charlotte, it's you. What a tease," she groaned.

Though Charlotte Woodward was eighteen to Josie's fourteen, she was smaller and slighter. She was a strong-willed girl with a peppery disposition. Maybe that was why Josie always thought of her as a redhead, though her hair was more gold than red. Charlotte had been Josie's teacher, and friend too. She had watched out for Josie ever since Josie had left school. Knowing how the younger girl loved to read, Charlotte supplied her with books from the library and encouraged her to study. Josie thought Charlotte was the most generous person she knew.

"I'm through at the bakery for the day. We baked thirty-five blueberry pies since four this morning, and I think I'll be blue until Christmas." Charlotte laughed. She held up arms that were stained almost to the elbows. Charlotte had taught for a year, Then, with the need to make more money, she had gone to work at the local bakery.

Josie covered her mouth with her hand. "Oh, Charlotte, you came for your *Ivanhoe*, and I forgot it," she exclaimed. Her face burned red. *Ivanhoe* cost six cents a week to borrow from the library and she had left it in the hayloft with her mother's dress and bonnet.

"Just as long as I have it when you're finished — Why, what an awful lump, and your eye. . . ." Charlotte stared at Josie.

Josie wiped her face with the damp cloth as if to wipe away the bruise. "I tripped and fell against a table when I was home, that's all. I'm fine," she said curtly. Wouldn't *anyone* leave her eye alone?

Charlotte put her arm around her friend's shoulders. "You don't have to make up stories for me," she said. "I know all about your uncle's drinking. Did he hurt your mother too?"

Josie swallowed hard. She wanted to share her fears with someone but hesitated to speak out, even to Charlotte. "Some, but not bad. And he was sorry this morning, he really was," she answered.

"Did your uncle push you against the table to give you such a lump"? Charlotte pressed.

"I told you I fell," Josie replied, but her voice sounded uncertain.

"He struck you." Charlotte tried another tack. "That's it, isn't it? He hit you." It wasn't a question.

In a way Josie felt relieved. "With his walking cane," she admitted. "He hit me on the arm, and that's when I fell. But he was sorry this morning. He came to my room to apologize."

"It's happened before, hasn't it?" Charlotte demanded.

"I-I . . . guess so." Josie was suddenly concerned about Charlotte's questioning.

"I've thought for a long time someone should know what that man is up to," Charlotte said, her voice crisp. It was the tone she had used to control the unruly boys in school, and it had never failed her yet.

"It won't happen again. I know it won't," Josie said.

Charlotte threw back her shoulders and put her hands on her hips in a way that Josie knew meant business. "It had better not," she snapped, "and just to make sure it doesn't, we'll go down to the courthouse and talk to Sheriff Chapman. You can tell him what you just told me."

"Oh, no, Charlotte, I couldn't," Josie sputtered. "It would make trouble. . . . Uncle Hiram would be furious — "

"Then I'll go to the courthouse myself. There must be some legal steps the sheriff can take," Charlotte interrupted.

"Please don't, Charlotte, I mean it," Josie grabbed Charlotte's arm.

"Something has to be done about your uncle, and if you won't do it, I will," Charlotte declared. She loosened her arm from Josie's grasp and started around the side of the house.

"Charlotte, please, you don't understand what Uncle Hiram would do to Ma if the sheriff went out there . . ." Josie begged.

But she was protesting to Charlotte's straight and determined back. Frantic, Josie raced after

Charlotte and seized her arm again. As Charlotte impatiently pulled away, Josie was aware of her friend's wiry strength.

"Now listen, Josie, this isn't just for your good. It's for the good of your whole family. No one has the right to hurt another person, wife, daughter, or anyone." Charlotte's brown eyes blazed. "Now you can't stop me, so don't try."

"But. . . ."

Charlotte turned away and even her skirts looked defiant as she rounded the corner of the house. Josie knew there was no point in saying more. With a moan, she sank down under the tree again and slapped the wet cloth back over her eyes.

The Newspaper Article

"Josie, I'm back, where are you?" Mrs. Brown's voice called out from the kitchen, and Josie hurried in, closing the door behind her to keep out the flies. Why she bothered she didn't know. The kitchen was already full of flies attracted to the sugar and spices of the pickles. The paper fly cage that hung from the ceiling did no good at all, and the flies buzzed annoyingly.

"Start fixing the fish, Josie, while I pluck and dress the goose. With you gone tomorrow, I don't want to spend the day cooking," Mrs. Brown said, tying on her apron.

Josie flipped over the lake trout Mrs. Brown had just bought and began to scale it. But with Charlotte on her mind, she was all thumbs. She knicked her finger with the knife deep enought to draw blood. When she turned her back to find a cloth to wrap it in, the Brown's cat leaped on the table, and Mrs. Brown rescued the fish just in time. After Josie finished the fish, she started to fill the pickle kegs. As she carried a potful of pickles across the kitchen, the cat ran between her legs, and the whole pot slid out of her hands, flooding the floor.

All the time she was mopping up the sticky mess, Will was in and out of the kitchen. First he begged for a slice of hot bread. Five minutes later he brought in his pet rabbit to feed him a carrot. Then he rode his hobbyhorse back and forth across the damp floor. With every slam of the back door, Josie flinched, sure it was Charlotte, back from the courthouse.

Charlotte had been gone for hours. Josie had prepared the noonday dinner, served it, and cleaned up, and still Charlotte hadn't returned. Where could she be? Josie didn't dare let herself think what would happen if Charlotte had persuaded the sheriff to go out to the farm. Just the thought of what Uncle Hiram might do made her shudder.

Josie had just begun the bread pudding for supper when there was a light tap at the door. Will never knocked. Certain that Charlotte was back, Josie raced to open it. But when she saw the thin, dark face of Mrs. McClintock, she was so surprised, she just stared. Mrs. McClintock, the druggist's wife, lived a few houses down the street.

"Afternoon, Mrs. McClintock. Mrs. Brown is upstairs," Josie finally said. "I'll fetch her."

"No, Josie, it's thee I want to see," Mrs. McClintock replied. Looking cool and crisp in her white Quaker kerchief and cap, she stepped into the kitchen.

"As I recall, the third Sunday of the month is thy free day, Josie, and on the morrow I find myself in a predicament," Mrs. McClintock began with such a sweet smile Josie was sure she wanted a favor. Josie held her breath. Tomorrow was *her* day. "In the morning, I have four ladies coming to my house for a meeting," Mrs. McClintock went on. "It's important that we be undisturbed, so I'd like help with refreshments and in the kitchen. I don't know how long the ladies will stay, but I would pay thee a half dollar, no matter how long or short their visit. And I would be much obliged."

A half dollar was almost a full week's wages from the Browns! But Josie had planned the day to herself . . . still, a half dollar that her uncle would know nothing about . . . and it would pay steamboat fare up Seneca Lake on her next free day. . . .

"I'll come, Mrs. McClintock, and I thank you for thinking of me," Josie said eagerly.

"Can thou come before eight to tidy the house . . . ."

"Mary Ann McClintock, what are you doing in my hot kitchen?" Mrs. Brown had entered the kitchen behind Josie. "Come into the front room and Josie can bring us lemonade."

"I thank thee, Rhoda, but it's Josie I came to see," Mrs. McClintock said with her gentle smile. As Josie wiped her sweaty face with the corner of her apron, she wondered if Quakers ever got hot, or even looked hot, for that matter. She wished she had redone her hair earlier.

"You came to see Josie?" Mrs. Brown raised her eyebrows.

"I'm having a meeting in the morning, and Josie has agreed to help me," Mrs. McClintock explained. "Four ladies are coming to my house. Maybe thou has heard of one of them, Mrs. Lucretia Mott of Philadelphia."

"Is that Mrs. Mott, the agitator?" Mrs. Brown asked sharply.

"Mrs. Mott, the reformer," Mrs. McClintock corrected. "She is only interested in improving the human condition, whether it's the ending of slavery or the bettering of woman's lot."

Mrs. Brown frowned. "I shouldn't think you would want to associate with such a person.

People like to gossip, and Mrs. Mott has a reputation as a troublemaker," she said. She drew herself up to her full impressive stature. "Besides, God created woman to serve her husband and childern, and she has no higher calling in life."

Josie bit her lip to keep a serious face. Mrs. Brown frequently raised her voice to heaven for the Almighty to witness what she went through with Mr. Brown and young Will.

"But I'd like to go, Mrs. Brown," Josie interjected. "And Mrs. McClintock offered to pay me generously."

Mrs. Brown looked at Josie. Her posture relaxed, and her face softened. "You could use the money, couldn't you, Josie?" she asked. "And don't let that uncle of yours get his hands on it, either."

Mrs. McClintock edged toward the back door. "I'll expect thee at eight, Josie," she called.

Mrs. Brown closed the door and turned to Josie. "The only reason I'm letting you work for that woman and be exposed to her radical friends is that you had already accepted her offer. Where you should be is in bed. You look poorly as an ailing cat, Josie, especially with that eye," she remarked. "As a matter of fact, why don't you work for Mrs. McClintock tomorrow, and plan to take your free day on Monday? That way you'll get a little rest."

Now Josie would have the money and the time to go up Seneca Lake! "Oh, thank you, Mrs. Brown, I . . . ."

Mrs. Brown held up her hand. "On the condition you take Will for the day," she continued. "I'm visiting my aunt on Monday, and I don't need Will around raising the devil."

Josie wouldn't have the quiet day she planned on, but Will would be in seventh heaven on a steamboat. "I'd be glad to take Will. Maybe he'd like a steamboat ride up Seneca Lake for a picnic. He's talked of it often enough," Josie suggested as if the idea had just occurred to her.

"That would suit Will, I'm sure," Mrs. Brown said, "and so long as you keep a close eye on him, it's agreeable with me."

With the trip on Josie's mind, as well as Charlotte, the rest of the day dragged. After she finished the bread pudding, she polished Mrs. Brown's new flat silver plate. It was so beautiful she usually enjoyed cleaning it, but today she dropped one piece after another. And when she started the ironing, her head and arm began to ache again. Someday she would weigh the heavy flatirons. Now at the end of the day as she warmed one flatiron on the stove while she ironed with the other, she would have wagered they each weighed five pounds. Her arm hurt from her shoulder to her wrist. When she pressed the last of Mrs. Brown's voluminous petticoats, she placed both irons back on the stove to reheat and leaned against the board to rest.

"Josie, it's me. I'm back," came a voice, and the back door swung open.

This time it *was* Charlotte. Josie's hand flew to her mouth. "Come in. I'm alone," she called out. Mrs. Brown was visiting a neighbor, and Will had fallen asleep in an exhausted heap on his bed.

Charlotte strode into the kitchen in her usual purposeful way. She waved a newspaper in front of her. "Look at this, Josie. If this doesn't beat all," she crowed. As she opened the newspaper on the ironing board, Josie quickly snatched the still-warm petticoat from under it.

"What about the sheriff, Charlotte? You didn't go to him, did you?" she asked, hoping against hope.

"Of course I went. I said I would, didn't I?" Charlotte retorted. "I marched right down to the courthouse and told Sheriff Chapman all about your uncle, for what little good it did. Now read this, Josie," she said again, pointing to an article in the newspaper.

"But Charlotte, wh-wh-what did the sheriff say?" Josie wasn't sure she wanted to hear the answer.

"Nothing, absolutely nothing. He tapped his fingers together in a spire and announced there was nothing to be done," Charlotte said. "I even asked if you should come down and explain what happened. He said not to bother, that it was none of the law's business what a man did to his wife and children, and none of my business either. He told me to tend to my baking." Charlotte snapped her fingers. "That for the sheriff," she said.

So Charlotte hadn't dragged Sheriff Chapman out to the farm. Josie closed her eyes and took a deep breath. "Thank heavens," she murmured.

"Even if a woman can't take a case to court, at least Sheriff Chapman might have put the fear of the Lord in Hiram Dexter's heart," Charlotte said.

"But I told you what terrible trouble it would have caused if the sheriff had gone to the farm," Josie said with feeling.

"Well, some good might come out of this anyway." Charlotte pointed to her paper again. "Maybe this is the answer to your problems."

"What?" Josie asked. She picked up Thursday's Seneca County Courier.

WOMAN'S RIGHTS CONVENTION —
A convention to discuss the social, civil, and religious rights of woman will be held in the Wesleyan Chapel at Seneca Falls, N.Y., on the 19th and 20th of July, current, commencing at ten o'clock A.M. During the first day the meeting will be exclusively for women, who are earnestly invited to attend. The public generally are invited to be present on the second day, when Lucretia Mott of Philadelphia and other ladies and gentlemen will address the convention.

Josie laughed out loud. "What silly idea do you have now? You're as crazy as Mrs. Abbott. She's all excited about this meeting too. I suppose you plan to go all the way to Seneca Falls?"

"Seneca Falls is only three and a half miles, not three hundred, and I'll be first in line waiting to get in," Charlotte replied. "If you have a grain of sense, you'll come with me."

Josie tried not to laugh again. "After I see what luck you had with the sheriff, I'm not sure I'd leave the betterment of women's fate up to you," she said.

"Joke if you want, Josie, but you just don't know what's good for you," Charlotte snapped as she folded her newspaper and started toward the back door. "I already have a half dozen girls lined up, so whether you join us or not doesn't matter to me," she said. "Let your uncle ruin your life, for all I care."

"I've almost finished *Ivanhoe*. I'll bring it back as soon as I fetch it from the farm," Josie shouted just before Charlotte slammed the door.

But as Josie returned to her ironing, she remembered what Mrs. McClintock had said. Wasn't Lucretia Mott one of the ladies who would be at her house tomorrow? Perhaps they were meeting to plan the convention. Josie shrugged her shoulders. What did it matter if President Polk were there, so long as she did her work and got paid her wages?

Meddling Women

Saturday's terrible heat had lifted by Sunday, but a leaden humidity lingered in the still air. If only it doesn't rain for our trip tomorrow, Josie thought as she dusted and straightened Mrs. McClintock's already-spotless house. She flicked the feather duster over the bookcase. Never had she seen so many books. On the farm, they had only a Bible and an almanac. Even the Browns owned only four books, none of which they ever opened.

Josie ran her fingers over Mrs. McClintock's well-worn library. Travel books, volumes of Shakespeare, even novels, *Vanity Fair*, *Oliver Twist*, *The Leatherstocking Tales*. And Thomas Nuttall's manual on land birds! Josie slipped out the famous handbook on birds and turned to the first page. "Of all classes of animals by which we are surrounded in the ample field of Nature, there are none more remarkable in their appearance and habits than the feathered inhabitants of the air," she read. The dusting was forgotten.

"What book interests thee so?" Mrs. McClintock had come into the room without Josie hearing her.

Embarrassed, Josie quickly closed the book. "Nuttall's *Manual of Ornithology*," she replied.

"Does thou like birds?" Mrs. McClintock asked.

"Oh, yes," Josie answered enthusiastically. "Someday I'd like to read this book through. And study Mr. Nuttall's beautiful pictures."

"Perhaps thou would like to borrow the book now?" Mrs. McClintock suggested.

"Oh, I would!" Josie said, "and I'd be very careful of it."

What a lucky day this turned out to be. The loan of this wonderful book and fifty cents. In high spirits, Josie swept the kitchen floor and put the teakettle on to boil. Maybe she could even snatch a few minutes to read while the women were busy.

Josie opened the door for Mrs. McClintock's guests. Mrs. Hunt of Waterloo was the only one she knew, but she guessed that the oldest of the four women, a delicate lady in gray Quaker silk and a prim white cap, was probably Mrs. Mott.

"Josie, please use the Imperial tea, and bring the tea tray to the parlor when it's ready,"

Mrs. McClintock said as she led her guests to the front room.

Before Josie arranged Mrs. McClintock's best blue china teacups on a tray, she laid the book on the kitchen windowsill out of harm's way. She ran her hand over its green leather cover. Hers to borrow.

There was scarcely room for the tray on Mrs. McClintock's sturdy center table. Papers, books, pamphlets, and a Bible were strewn from one end of the mahogany table to the other.

"Nobody wants to attend a convention just to hear a lot of complaints," Mrs. McClintock was saying. "Here, Josie, just set the tea things here. . . ." She cleared a space for the tray.

"I wonder how many women will come. Haying season is a hard time for women to be away from home," said the lady Josie guessed was Mrs. Mott.

Mrs. McClintock put her hand on Josie's arm. "Mrs. Stanton would prefer lemonade, Josie, if thou would make some for her, please," she said.

No time to read now. Josie looked longingly at the book on the windowsill as she headed for the cold cellar to hunt up the lemons. Later perhaps. After all, how much tea and lemonade could five ladies drink? While Josie

squeezed the juice into a tall pitcher, she thought about Mrs. McClintock's guests. They were discussing the Woman's Rights Convention.

Yesterday she had thought the idea was silly. Now she wasn't so sure. What would Uncle Hiram think if her mother went to the convention as Mrs. Abbott wanted her to? He'd be angry, that's what. Even good-natured Mr. Brown probably wouldn't like the idea. No, both men, different as they were, would be unhappy with their wives going off to a Woman's Rights Convention. But somehow, that didn't seem fair either, Josie thought.

Josie dropped fresh mint leaves in the lemonade pitcher and placed it on the tray with a tumbler. When she entered the parlor, the women were deep in discussion.

"But trying to get the vote for women will make people so angry they won't listen to anything else we have to say," Mrs. Hunt said. Josie tried to guess which one was Mrs. Stanton without interrupting.

"Aye, Lizzie, thou will make us ridiculous," Mrs. Mott agreed.

Josie decided that Mrs. Stanton was the plump, pleasant-looking matron, the only one without a teacup at her place. And the only one not in Quaker gray. She lowered the tray beside her.

"But with the vote, women can help change the laws. If we have to live by the laws, we should have a say in what they are," Mrs. Stanton responded. She didn't notice the tray beside her. "Our property is taxed, but we have no voice in how our money is spent." Mrs. Stanton raised her hand for emphasis, and her arm knocked against the pitcher. Over it went with a crash, the lemonade spreading across the table, flooding the papers and books, then running down onto Mrs. McClintock's carpet.

"Oh, I'm so sorry." Mrs. Stanton jumped up as the sticky lemonade dripped into her lap.

"Dear me. Josie, quickly, get some clean cloths," Mrs. McClintock ordered.

"It was my fa-fa-fault," Josie stammered. She dashed into the kitchen for rags and a mop. When she returned, the women were all on their feet, shaking the papers and books and drying them with their napkins. Josie handed Mrs. Stanton a clean rag, then stooped and blotted up the worst of the lemonade on the carpet. With fresh rags, she wiped the table.

"I'm s-sorry," she stuttered again. How could she have been so careless? Mrs. McClintock wouldn't think her help was worth a ha'penny, let alone a half dollar.

"Nonsense, child, it was more my fault than yours," Mrs. Stanton said as she knelt beside Josie to help mop up the lemonade. An impish grin lit her round face. "I never cry over spilt lemonade," she giggled. They both stood up. Mrs. Stanton was six inches shorter and had to tilt her head to look up at Josie.

"Your first name's Josie, I know, but what's your surname?" she asked.

"Josephine Dexter," Josie replied.

"Well, you and I made quite a puddle, didn't we, Josephine?" Mrs. Stanton smiled. Then she looked at Josie more closely. "Your eye?" She made it sound like a question. "What a bad bruise."

Josie blushed, embarrassed all over again. The women all stared at her. If only the floor would open up and let her drop through. "I tripped and fell," she blurted out.

"I haven't seen you here before, Josephine. Where do you live?" Mrs. Stanton asked. The other women were still listening.

"I hire out to the Browns' down the street and board there," Josie answered, making an effort not to stammer. How could one black eye cause so much trouble?

"Thy stepfather is Hiram Dexter, isn't he?" Mrs. Hunt asked. "I've known Hiram for years. He did well with his canalboat, as I recall. Then he had that terrible accident. When did he take over thy farm, Josephine?"

"Five years ago, when my father died. Then he married my mother," Josie mumbled.

"I saw Hiram Dexter in town not long ago," Mrs. McClintock said. "He'd been drinking."

"Did your uncle do that to your eye?" Mrs. Stanton asked. She was as persistent as a dog with a bone.

"No, not exactly . . . my uncle and I had some words, that's all . . . it was an accident that I fell . . . really . . ." Josie repeated.

Mrs. Stanton ignored Josie's denial. "That's dreadful," she commented. "Children are the father's property just like the family cow, no matter how he treats them. That, ladies, is why women need the vote. Just the way the American colonies drew up the Declaration of Independence from Great Britain, so we must draw up our Declaration of Independence from men. . . ."

"Lizzie, enough preaching. We have work to do," Mrs. Mott interrupted. "Save thy speeches for the convention."

The other women had seated themselves

again and were riffling through their papers and books, no longer listening to Mrs. Stanton. She took a deep breath as if to go on, then threw back her head. Her laugh filled the parlor.

"Once I get started, Josephine, I'm like a spring freshet that can't be dammed up," she said. As she sat down at the table, she reached for a pamphlet. "I should have thought of that before. The Declaration of Independence should be our guide."

Josie gathered up the soiled napkins and the empty teacups and saucers and stacked them haphazardly on the tray. She almost ran with them into the kitchen. She slid the tray onto the kitchen table and grabbed a chair to steady herself. What had she gotten into? She was supposed to help with refreshments, not get involved in the discussion. If only she hadn't been so greedy for that half dollar, she could be off now, enjoying her free day.

Josie sat in the kitchen a long time. The longer she sat, the angrier she became. Talk about rights. What right had these women to pry and snoop? They were as bad as Mrs. Abbott and Charlotte with their nosy questions. She wanted no part of their meddling. Uncle Hiram was her problem, not theirs. All she wanted was to be left alone, to manage her own life as she saw fit. Determined to put everything else from her mind, she took Mrs. McClintock's book from the windowsill and began to read.

"Didn't thou hear me call?" Mrs. McClintock stood in the open kitchen door. Her voice was sharper than usual. "We'd like fresh tea in the parlor, please."

Josie slipped the book behind her back and stood up. "Oh, yes, ma'am, I'm sorry," she replied. She had been no help at all today.

Quickly she cut fresh raisin bread and spread thick peach jam on each slice. While the water for the tea was heating, Josie stepped outside and snipped five rose blossoms from Mrs. McClintock's climbing rose bush. Maybe their sweet fragrance would please the women.

But they were working hard and didn't even notice the roses Josie had tucked in each napkin or the sugar-coated mint leaves that sweetened their tea.

"Now don't forget, Josephine," Mrs. Stanton said. She put her hand on Josie's arm.

Oh, no, not again, Josie groaned inwardly. "Forget what, ma'am?" she asked aloud.

"Why, to come to our convention Wednesday next, of course, so you can sign our Declaration," Mrs. Stanton replied. "We'll need all the support we can get."

This time Josie just nodded and smiled. Mrs.

Stanton released her sleeve, and Josie hurried from the parlor. Sign indeed. The closest she would be to Seneca Falls on Wednesday would be Mrs. Brown's kitchen in Waterloo, a safe three miles away.

An Argument

Monday dawned clear and fair. A before-dawn thunderstorm had left the air cool and dry. And Mr. Brown, with bank business in Geneva, promised to drive Josie and Will right to the steamboat landing for their big day.

Best of all, Sunday at Mrs. McClintock's had ended on a good note. Several men had joined the women in the afternoon, and they had all stayed late. They had been so excited about the convention they had scarcely noticed Josie again. She, in turn, stayed close to the kitchen. There had even been enough free time to read well into Mr. Nuttall's manual.

Josie and Will were up by dawn on Monday morning, Will to fix his fishing pole and dig worms for bait, and Josie to pack their picnic. Carefully wrapping Mrs. McClintock's book in newspaper, she tucked it in the bottom of the basket for reading on the boat.

As they rode along the turnpike toward Geneva in the early-morning quietness, Josie thought how curious it felt to be driven like a lady in a buggy, instead of baking morning pies, or tending the garden, or feeding the pigs. Maybe part of the strangeness came from wearing one of Mrs. Brown's cast-off dresses, a yellow gingham that had been cut down to fit.

"When will we get there, Papa? How big is the boat? How fast will it go?" Will kept up a steady barrage of questions.

"Enough, Will, you're worse than a magpie," Mr. Brown said. His tone was stern, but he smiled and patted his son's knee.

"You're so busy talking, I bet you didn't even notice that doe and her fawn backaways," Josie said as they bounced along the hard-packed dirt road. "And look over there at that flock of blackbirds. Sometimes there are hundreds and hundreds of birds in those flocks."

They all looked up at the red-winged blackbirds that flew in the clear sky west of the turnpike. "You're quite an authority on birds, aren't you, Josie?" Mr. Brown observed.

Josie hadn't thought of it that way before, but she realized that over the years she *had* learned a lot about birds. And, with the help of Mr. Nuttall's book, was learning even more. "I guess that's true, Mr. Brown," she acknowledged.

"Chuck, chuck." The air was filled with the blackbirds' throaty call as they wheeled and turned in unison. More and more birds joined the flock until it looked like a giant black cloak billowing in the sky. There must have been thousands of them, impressing even Will into silence.

When they reached the steamboat landing, Josie and Will climbed down from the buggy. "Will is only half fare, Josie, so here's the money for his pass," Mr. Brown said. He selected two shillings from his purse. His fingers hesitated over the other coins for a moment. Then he pulled out two quarters and gave them to Josie. "For your fare," he said gruffly. He clucked at his horse, and the buggy was gone before Josie could thank him.

She stared at the quarters. In two days she'd collected a whole dollar! "Your papa is certainly generous," she said to Will as they headed for the steamboat office.

After they bought their passes, they walked out on the hundred-yard-long jetty that stretched into Seneca Lake. The steamboat, *Richard Stevens*, was docked at the end of it. Though the early-morning mist from the lake folded ghost-like around her silhouette, there was bustling activity everywhere. Passengers had begun to arrive. Workers scurried on her decks, and a thin plume of smoke curled from her narrow smokestack as the engineers began to stoke her fires. The gulls already circled and dipped above her, squawking in anticipation of scraps.

Will fairly danced up and down with excitement. He had insisted on wearing his sailor suit, and in his blue blouse and blue pie cap, he had never looked more appealing. "Can't we get on the boat yet, Josie?" he begged.

Josie's arm hurt from carrying the heavy picnic basket, and she lowered it to the dock. "Not until they put down the gangplank, Will. See there's no way for us to get on board," she pointed out.

A small knot of passengers stood around them. Like Josie and Will, the early arrivals were enjoying the scene.

"Isn't that little Master William Brown?" a voice asked. Josie and Will turned around. It was Mr. Hubbard from Merrill's Cash and Tea Store in Waterloo, standing by a big wheelbarrow. "Good morning, William," he said with a smile at Will and a nod in Josie's direction.

"Will, say good morning to Mr. Hubbard," Josie prompted.

"Morning," Will answered with a cheerful

grin. "Are you going on a picnic today too?"

Mr. Hubbard laughed. "No, there's little time for picnics when you reach my age, William." He pointed to his wheelbarrow. "I'm just waiting to unload some bolts of dress goods from the boat. Then I'm headed back to the store."

"Josie doesn't need dress goods. She wears my mama's dresses," Will boasted. He held out his fishing pole. "Josie and me are going to Lodi Landing and hike to the falls, and I'm going fishing. Josie, how long will it take to get to Lodi Landing?" Will asked without stopping to catch his breath.

Josie was still recovering from Will's remark about her dress when Mr. Hubbard spoke up. "Now, William, you must learn to do your sums just like your father does," he said. "It's about eighteen miles to Lodi Landing. Since there's two knots to a mile and the boat runs eleven or twelve knots, that would take . . . let me see . . . allowing for stops . . . close to three hours."

Mr. Hubbard was wrong. Josie had just read a library book that was full of nautical facts. "I believe a knot is closer in distance to a mile, sir, rather than two," she said. "The trip to Lodi Landing should take nearer an hour and a half than three."

Mr. Hubbard looked at Josie as if she had just stepped on his foot. "Nonsense," he contradicted. His scrawny neck quivered like a turkey gobbler's. "A knot is equal to two miles, no more, no less."

He paused, and Josie knew he was waiting for her to back down. She started to speak, to admit he was right. Then she changed her mind. Mr. Hubbard wasn't right. But rather than argue, she tried to change the subject. Out of the corner of her eye she noticed the gangplank was down and the deckhands had started to unload the freight. "Look, sir, there's the freight. Perhaps your dress goods are ready," she said.

Without comment, Mr. Hubbard lifted his wheelbarrow. As Josie picked up her picnic basket to follow him to the boat, a hand reached around her and tapped Mr. Hubbard on the arm. "You there, you oughta listen to the young lady. She's right. A knot is far closer to a land mile than two," a young man with a full mustache said loudly.

Mr. Hubbard spun around at the voice and glared at the man behind Josie. "Why, you're wrong," he exclaimed. "I've traveled on boats and know what I'm talking about."

The young man smiled. "I crewed on ships

six years, so don't tell me *I* don't know what I'm talking about. One knot, one mile, or nearly so," he said pleasantly. He was smoking a strange wooden pipe. The end of the pipe was a carved frog, its wide mouth the bowl. Will stared at it, fascinated.

"That's your opinion only," Mr. Hubbard retorted. "I stand by my statement."

Josie and Will were caught between the two men. Josie scrunched up her shoulders and wished she could disappear as the other passengers sensed an argument and turned in their direction.

"It doesn't matter," she said. If the two men heard her, they didn't pay any attention.

"Look, there's the captain," the young man said as a blue-uniformed figure strode over the gangplank onto the dock. "Captain, sir, over here," he called. He waved to the captain.

"We'd like a dispute settled for us, Captain," Mr. Hubbard said when the officer had reached them. Though Mr. Hubbard's words were polite, he was scowling. "A knot is equal in distance to two miles, is it not, sir?"

The captain chuckled. "I hope not. I've been on the water twenty years, and if that were true, I'd have sailed almost twice as far as I thought I had," he answered. "A knot is only eight hundred feet more than a mile.''

There was a small burst of laughter, and Josie realized they were surrounded by interested listeners. The young man guffawed and winked at Josie. ''The young miss was right after all. I'm just sorry I didn't take a wager on it. Wal, some folks don't know their bow from their stern and need a female to tell'em,'' he joked. He pushed his way through the smiling spectators and was gone.

The brass bell on the *Richard Stevens* suddenly clanged, and the crowd, still laughing, began to head for the gangplank. Mr. Hubbard didn't say a word, but Josie could feel his anger wash over her. She smiled tentatively. He probably expected an apology. But she wouldn't give one. After all, she had been right. But her good humor seemed to infuriate him, and she could hear him muttering under his breath as she prodded Will toward the boat.

''C'mon, Will, let's board the boat and find a seat. This basket is heavy,'' she said. She tried to put Mr. Hubbard from her mind.

''Josie, when are we going to start? Soon?'' Will asked as they crossed the gangplank and stepped onto the deck of the *Richard Stevens*. Will's sailor cap was already askew, and his white trousers were dirty.

Josie straightened his cap and brushed off his pants. "I think there will be some whistles, Will, and then we'll start," she replied. She looked over the railing down at the dock. Perhaps that young man was still there. She wondered why he smoked such an odd-looking pipe. She had never seen one like it.

Josie didn't spot him, but she did see Mr. Hubbard. He was angrily slapping bolts of dress goods into his wheelbarrow. Josie felt sorry for him, but it wasn't her fault he looked the dunce. He should have known his facts before he spouted them.

Will jumped on the first rung of the railing and reached over to hug her. "You were right about that knot and mile stuff, weren't you, Josie?" he asked.

"Aye, I was," she answered with satisfaction. "And I didn't back down." She savored the new and pleasant sensation a moment before she took Will's hand to find their seats.

Josie Takes a Plunge

Josie chose a bench toward the bow, under a big life preserver that read *Richard Stevens, Seneca Lake Steam Navigation Company*. Not that she was worried about an accident, but after all, she was responsible for Will. Before she slipped the picnic basket and Will's fishing pole beneath the bench, she reached in and took out Mr. Nuttall's manual. Carefully, she unwrapped its newspaper covering and, just for fun, turned to the section on red-winged blackbirds.

But it was hard to read with Will jumping up and down, running over to the railing and back, exclaiming over every new arrival.

"Look at that lady with the big red nose, Josie," Will called out. He pointed to a boarding passenger. Josie was too embarrassed to do more than glance up as a heavyset woman passed by. Her nose really did look red. Josie tried not to giggle as she held the book up in front of her face.

She went back to her reading. "About the

end of April or early in May, in the middle and northern parts of the Union, the Red-Winged Blackbirds commence constructing their nests. . . ."

Will tugged at Josie's arm to get her attention. "What is it, Will?" She couldn't help being annoyed.

"You got to come, Josie," Will insisted. "There's the hugest goat I ever saw coming on the boat." His cheeks were pink with excitement, and his eyes sparkled. Josie couldn't resist him.

"All right," she said, "but if I come, he'd better be the biggest goat in the whole wide world."

"He is," Will answered solemnly.

Josie put a marker in her book and slipped it in the basket. Holding Will's hand, she walked to the boat's railing.

"There's the goat, Josie." Will pointed down to the dock where a farmer was leading a huge billy goat by a rope toward the boat. Will was right. Even from where they stood on the deck of the *Richard Stevens*, the goat looked as big as a Shetland pony. If he stood on his hind legs, Josie guessed he would be taller than a man. Even Mr. Hubbard, who had finished loading his wheelbarrow, stared at the farmer and his goat as they passed him on the dock.

"Hey, Jake, you gonna take that billy goat up to Jefferson and try to sell him where they never heard of him?" A man leaning on the railing next to Josie shouted down to the farmer. He nudged his companion. "Jake's been trying to sell that mean old he-goat for a year. Every time Jake gets rid of him he gets brung back."

They watched the farmer hand his pass to the ticket collector. But as he started up the gangplank, the big animal dug in his four heels, and the rope snapped taut. The farmer pulled on the rope, but the harder he tugged, the more the goat refused to budge.

"Beh-h-h," they heard the goat blat his disdain. He lifted his lip in a sneer as the furious farmer alternately pulled and wooed him toward the gangplank.

There was a blast of the whistle, and the boat trembled under her powerful head of steam. Will squirmed beside Josie. "Are we going to leave without the goat?" He sounded worried. "He'd come on the boat if he had something to eat, I bet."

"Mmm," Josie answered, not paying much attention. She was watching the farmer. He tied the animal to a snubbing post on the dock, then ran up the gangplank onto the boat. Quite a crowd had gathered by the railing, but they parted good-naturedly as the farmer shouldered his way toward the hold.

Josie lost interest. He was probably going for food. Or a stick. She didn't wait to find out. She made her way back to the bench and sat down, anxious to get on with her book. There was so much to learn. Mr. Nuttall knew just about everything there was to know about birds. How wonderful it would be to travel and sketch and write as he did. She tucked her feet up under her skirts and started to read again. She hardly noticed Will pull out the picnic basket and rustle through it.

"Don't eat everything," she murmured without lifting her eyes from her book. She finished the section on red-winged blackbirds.

"Hey, looky that boy. He'll get hurt. That's a mean goat," Josie heard someone call out. Even before her mind took in the words, she was on her feet, shoving her way to the ship's railing. She looked down. There was Will in his blue and white sailor suit on the dock. With one hand he grasped the goat's rope, and with the other he held out a piece of cold chicken from the picnic basket.

The goat gobbled down the chicken in one bite; then he took a step backwards, lowering his head at Will. His shiny horns swept back like great spears.

Josie leaned over the boat's railing. "Wi — " she started to shout. Before the word was out, she realized her mistake. She didn't want to startle either Will or the goat. The other passengers must have felt the same way. There was an instant silence as everyone froze in horror. Now that Will was so close to the goat, he seemed to be having second thoughts himself. He dropped the rope and inched his left foot back, then his right, retreating across the dock toward the gangplank.

"Beh-h-h," the goat blatted. He shook his wide horns.

Josie pushed her way through the bystanders and raced back to her seat. She snatched the tablecloth from the top of the picnic basket and ran back to the railing. She jumped on the gangplank and flew down it, stopping on the dock between Will and the goat.

"Run," she screamed at Will as she threw the tablecloth at the goat's head.

Will's little body darted behind Josie in a flash of blue and white. She heard him pound up the gangplank. And there she was on the dock with the goat. She had hoped to cover the animal's head with the tablecloth, but instead, had draped it over one horn. Though it had given Will time to get away, it had also enraged the goat. He quickly stepped between Josie and the safety of the gangplank.

"Beh-h-h," he bellowed again and started toward Josie.

There was nothing to do but run. As Josie started for the far side of the dock, she could hear the clatter of the goat's hooves loud as drumfire behind her. But the dock was wet, and Josie felt her feet slip out from under her. She tried to regain her balance. But it was too late. There was no way she could stop from sliding right off the dock into the lake. And in she went with a splash. The water, which had looked so sapphire blue from above, was murky green below. And the cold force of it snatched her breath away. She sank swiftly.

Josie had no idea the water would be so deep or that she would drop so quickly. It suddenly occurred to her that she might drown. Though she had never learned to swim, she knew there was something she should do. Kick. But her skirts twisted around her legs like ropes. Mustering all her strength, she freed her legs from her skirts and kicked. She kicked so

hard she felt her shoes flop off. But it worked. At least she seemed to rise upward, rather than sink downward. Just when she was certain her chest would explode her head broke the surface of the water.

"Help," she cried feebly. A dozen hands reached down and pulled her up. They dragged her along the rough wood of the dock and stretched her out on her stomach, where she lay wheezing.

"Josie, get up," she heard Will call. She felt his strong little fists pound into her back. "Get up," he demanded. His voice was shrill with fear.

"I'm all right, Will," Josie gasped, though she couldn't move a muscle. Someone rolled her over, but such a gush of water ran back down her throat she began to gag.

"Set her up," a man said, and arms propped her up. Someone else pounded her on the back, making her cough all the more.

"Enough," she croaked, waving her arms to stop the pounding. A ring of worried faces peered down at her. Even Mr. Hubbard looked concerned. Embarrassed by all the attention, Josie tried to smile.

"Look, she's gonna be fine," a man said. There was a relieved chorus of agreement.

Will leaned over her. "The man caught his goat," he said.

Josie nodded her head and gulped for air as if she could never get enough. The other passengers, seeing she was going to be all right, started back to the boat. A whistle tooted. It must be almost time to leave, Josie realized.

"Help me up, Will," she ordered and held out her hands. He manfully steadied her as she struggled to her feet, the water streaming off her like a waterfall. Though she felt light-headed, she wrung out her skirt and squeezed as much water as she could from her hair. Then she picked up Mrs. Brown's tablecloth from the dock and leaning on Will for support, headed for the *Richard Stevens*.

"Young lady, wait." It was Mr. Hubbard. "I got my wagon over to Castle Street," he said. His eyes looked everywhere but at Josie. "You and William can ride back to Waterloo with me." It was more of a command than an offer.

"Thank you, sir, but we intend to take our steamboat ride as we planned," Josie answered. Her voice was still shaky. If only she could get to her seat and sit down.

"But you can't board the boat in front of all those people like that," Mr. Hubbard protested.

Josie looked down at her dress. Her shoes were gone, and her stockings were ripped. And she was soaked, all right, so that her dress clung to her body like wet wallpaper. She suddenly wished she were flat-chested like Charlotte. instead of what her mother called full-busted. Still, it would take more than a dunking for Josie to back down now. Besides, it was a breezy clear day, and she would dry quickly.

Two deckhands began to uncleat the lines, and Josie knew in a minute the gangplank would go up. All the passengers had reboarded. Even the farmer and his now-docile goat had disappeared into the hold. Without bothering to answer Mr. Hubbard, Josie took Will's hand and hurried toward the boat. They dashed aboard the *Richard Stevens* just before the deckhands took up the gangplank.

The whistle tooted again, and the sidewheels turned slowly in reverse as the breast line went taut. The stern swung in. At a bell signal, a deckhand pulled up the last hawser and jumped nimbly on board with it. As a second bell sounded, the wheels turned forward. The captain pulled three times on the whistle cord, and the *Richard Stevens*' escort of gulls wheeled and called as she pulled from the dock.

"Good-bye, Mr. Hubbard." Will waved a

friendly farewell from the railing. Mr. Hubbard was just where they had left him on the dock. He was watching the boat, but he never answered Will's salute. He gave one last look, then stalked away.

Josie was too exhausted to care. She headed for their bench. All she wanted was rest. She found the bench easily enough, but dazed as she was, she realized something was wrong. It was the same bench where she had been sitting, with the same life preserver hanging above it. But the picnic basket and Will's fishing pole were gone. And even worse, so was Mrs. McClintock's book.

Cal Evans

Josie stared at the empty bench. There was nothing on it. Or under it. The book, the picnic basket, and the fishing pole were gone. She stooped down and peered under the bench. Then she searched the benches on either side. Someone must have picked up the basket by mistake. Or stolen it. How could Josie ever explain to Mrs. McClintock she had lost the book only the day after she had borrowed it? And Mrs. Brown would be furious if her picnic basket were missing.

Will wandered over. "What are you looking for, Josie?" he asked.

"The picnic basket and your fishing pole," Josie mumbled.

"You mean all our food is gone? And my fishing pole?" he demanded. His expression was stricken.

"I'll have to look for them," Josie said. And she knew that's what she would have to do no matter how she felt. Or how terrible she looked. Her dress clung to her like a second skin, outlining every curve, and her hair hung limp and damp from its knot. Everyone would stare. She couldn't do it. She just couldn't. But she knew she had to. And she had better begin.

"Will, you set right there on the bench in case someone returns our things. I'm going to hunt around the boat for them. Now *don't move.*" Josie spoke more curtly than she meant to.

Will plopped down on the bench and blinked at Josie with wide blue eyes. "But you don't have your shoes on," he said.

Josie looked down at her stockinged feet. She had forgotten her shoes were on the bottom of Seneca Lake. But there was no putting off her search, shoes or no shoes. She shook out her skirts and headed for a brightly dressed woman who stood by the railing. Josie had noticed her before. She was elaborately turned out in ruffles and ribbons and had snappy brown eyes that seemed to take in everything.

"I wonder, ma'am, if you've seen a picnic basket and a book and a fishing pole I've lost," Josie asked in a rush.

The woman studied Josie for a minute. "Is that all you've lost?" she retorted with a husky laugh.

The woman was about to say more when Josie noticed a deckhand passing by. She ran over to him. "Sir, wait," she called. "I'm the one who fell in the lake," she explained. "When I got back on board, everything I had with me was gone. Do you know where my things might be?"

The deckhand looked at Josie as if she had been dredged up from the bottom of Seneca Lake. "Not I," he said, "but if they turn up, I'll come find you."

No one seemed able to help. Maybe it would just be better to walk around the deck and try to spot the basket. And that meant everyone seeing her. Josie longed to run back to where she had left Will and sit with him until she dried. But the thought of the book and the basket kept her going. Especially the book. She just had to find it.

Never had Josie been the object of so much attention. Everyone turned to stare as she slowly walked the deck, poking under the benches, looking behind pillars, opening doors. Three ladies giggled under their black silk parasols when she passed them, and a young boy trailed her down the deck, chanting;

> Left foot — right foot —
>   Any foot at all.
> Sally lost her petticoat.
>   A' goin to the ball.

Josie cringed. If someone had spoken to her, she couldn't have answered for the tightness in her throat. And her head spun. But the farther she walked and the more people ogled, the more determined she was to find her belongings.

When she reached the bow of the boat, she glanced out over the lake. The *Richard Stevens* steamed through the water on a steady course. Josie had almost forgotten she was on a boat. She shivered as the lake breeze cut through her damp clothes and chilled her to the marrow. If only she could stand in the sun long enough to dry out. But there was no time now. She began her search again.

"Why, isn't that Rhoda Brown's hired girl?" A woman called out. Josie was crouched down, half under a bench. She forced herself to straighten up and smile.

"It *is* Rhoda Brown's girl. My goodness, what are you doing on this boat?" the woman demanded. It was Mrs. Jackman from Waterloo. Josie didn't recognize her long, rather handsome face so much as her piercing voice. It was shrill as a blue jay's.

"Morning, ma'am. I-I'm just looking for something," Josie tried to sound casual. It would never do to have Mrs. Jackman find out she had lost Mrs. Brown's picnic basket. Her tongue was not only sharp as a blue jay's, but just as busy.

"I'm on my way to Jefferson to pick up my sister at the train depot. Then I'm bringing her back on the return trip. If Mrs. Brown is aboard, we could sit together," Mrs. Jackman said.

"No, I'm alone with Will," Josie spoke carefully.

"But you're soaking wet. Whatever have you been doing, and where are your shoes?" Mrs. Jackman's voice crackled with curiosity.

Josie was very, very tired, and suddenly she didn't want to answer any more questions. "I must get back to Will," she said quietly. She walked past Mrs. Jackman without replying.

Josie heard Mrs. Jackman mumble something, but she didn't look back. It was true about Will. There was no telling what mischief he might be into by now. In her search, Josie had circled more than halfway around the boat. As she started to complete the circle, she was aware for the first time of the thrumming of the engine and the vibration of the deck under her feet. The huge wheels churned the clear water into sarsaparilla foam, and Josie realized that what was to have been her perfect day had started out just plain awful.

She looked out over the serene water. An

occasional fish broke the surface of the lake to leap at an insect, and the sun flashed through hoops of silver. In the distance, a huge fish-hawk skimmed the water's edge on wings equal to a man's height. On the lake banks, she could see rocky crags with jutting points and deep ravines, all softened by red cedar trees. But she was hardly aware of the lake's beauty. She leaned against a pillar and let the sun's warmth bake into her.

"Ain't you the girl that fell in the lake?" It was a man's voice behind her and a man's pipe smoke she smelled.

Josie didn't answer. If he persisted, she would just play dumb. She watched two gulls quarrel over a crust of bread tossed from the boat.

"I thought you wasn't going to board the boat," the man said. This time the pipe smoke nudged a memory. Josie turned and saw the young man who had taken her part against Mr. Hubbard. When the young man smiled, he seemed like an old friend. "I saw how you fell in the lake and figgered you wasn't coming back on board," he explained, "so when I spied your things, I picked 'em up. I was gonna bring 'em back to Geneva on the return trip."

The young man spoke so offhandedly it took Josie a moment to grasp his meaning. "You have my b-b-book?" And the basket?" she asked.

"Yep, right over there." The man waved his pipe behind him. Under a bench, Josie saw the edge of the basket. She ran to it. The book, the food, were all inside. Even Will's fishing pole was tucked safely out of sight.

Josie laughed out loud with relief. "They are here," she said. Her embarrassment had been worth it after all.

It was the young man's turn to laugh. "I guess you had a fright when you couldn't find 'em." he said. "But you looked like such a drowned cat I ne'er thought you'd board again."

Josie flapped her skirts. Slowly they were drying. "I shouldn't have, I guess, but Will and I had counted. . . ." Will! She had forgotten him again.

"Thank you so much, sir. I got to go. Will is by himself." Josie started to pick up the basket, but the man reached down and grabbed it first.

"I'll carry it for you," he said. "It's the least I can do after stealing it." He chuckled.

Will was right where Josie had left him,

his sailor cap over one eye, and his dirty cheeks streaked with tears. "Where were you?" He jumped up and threw his arms around Josie. "You didn't come back, and I was hungry," he cried. "I could smell food."

Josie gave him a hard hug. "You were such a good boy, you can have whatever you want to eat. This nice man found our basket," she said.

Will reached for his fishing pole and clutched it to him. "Can I have some cake?"

At Will's request, Josie had baked a watermelon cake for the picnic. It was a tinted sugar pink cake filled with raisins to look like seeds and frosted with white icing.

"I'm hungry as Will," Josie said. "Why don't I cut us all a piece?" She sliced three good-sized helpings, and they sat down together on the bench to eat.

"Wal, you two had a busy morning. Where you headed?" the young man said when he had finished. He filled his strange frog pipe with fresh tobacco. Will stared.

"Lodi Landing," Josie replied. "We're going to walk up Mill Creek to see the falls."

"Ain't never seen 'em, but I hear they're quite a sight," the young man said. He lit his pipe. "I'm disembarking there myself. I work over to the Smith Nursery in Geneva and got to go to Lodi about some complaints we got on an order of apple trees. We oughta be docking soon, as a matter of fact."

By the time Will had devoured another helping of cake, tried to lift the life preserver from its hook, and lost his cap overboard, the whistle had blown and the *Richard Stevens* was headed toward shore. The reversing side-wheels boiled up the blue water as her bow approached the dock, The brass bell clanged, the wheels stopped, and the whistle blew again as the gangplank came clattering out.

"Here, let me fetch your basket," the young man suggested. Carrying the picnic basket, Cal followed Josie and Will over the gangplank. They paused on the dock.

"Well, I thank you, Mr. . . . ah . . ." Josie realized she didn't know his name.

"Cal Evans," the young man said with a grin. His teeth were big and even and white under his dark mustache. For the first time Josie noticed his eyes as well. They were more green than blue, almost sea-colored.

"I'm Josie Dexter," she said, returning his smile. She felt no shyness with Cal the way she usually did with strangers.

"Well, Josie Dexter, I'll look forward to

seeing you on the return trip. You two can manage on your own from now on, I reckon. You're a spunky miss."

No one had ever called Josie spunky before. She blushed and straightened her shoulders. Being considered spunky was a new experience and she liked it.

There was a companionable silence as she and Will and Cal turned to watch the *Richard Stevens* draw away from the landing. But it was with a sudden shock that Josie recognized the tall, straight figure of Mrs. Jackman standing by the railing as the boat steamed away. There was no doubt in Josie's mind that Mrs. Jackman had seen the three of them get off together and was watching them still. Josie couldn't see Mrs. Jackman's expression, but she could guess what it would be. Grim. And disapproving.

Picnic

Josie, Will, and Cal stood on the dock until the boat had steamed out into the lake and Mrs. Jackman was too far away to see. Josie wondered if Mrs. Jackman was watching them fade into the distance, as Josie was watching her.

"Wal, I gotta get started for Lodi. Have a pleasant day, and I'll see you this afternoon. Farewell, Josie Dexter, and Will." Cal tipped his cap and headed for a dirt road that Josie hadn't even noticed.

Though he disappeared around a bend, the odor of his pipe smoke lingered. It was the only sign that he had even been there. Together Josie and Will watched the *Richard Stevens* steam out of sight, her final whistle echoing back across the water. They felt all alone in the vastness of the still lake and craggy shoreline.

"Is this the biggest lake in the world, Josie?" Will asked.

Josie laughed. "It's big, but not the biggest.

It's just one of the Finger Lakes. The Indians say the Great Spirit laid his hand on the land to bless it, and the imprint of his six fingers left the Finger Lakes. Seneca Lake is the longest middle finger," she explained.

Will's eyes grew round. "Are there Indians around here?"

"Not now, but the Iroquois used to live right where we're standing." Josie tapped the ground with her bare foot.

"Kyeek! Kyeek! Kyeek!" A fierce scream rent the air.

Will clutched his fishing pole and looked up at Josie. "Is that an Indian war cry?" he whispered.

"No, Will. It's only a bird," Josie explained. "If we're quiet, we might see it."

Will slowly turned his head and searched the towering trees behind him with a worried expression. From somewhere high above, a giant fish hawk swooped down toward the lake. Its sleek breast was so white it looked freshly laundered.

"It *is* a bird." Will laughed his relief.

"Kyeek! Kyeek!" the fish hawk cried again as it hovered over the water. Suddenly, it closed its long wings and plunged into the lake feet first, splashing up a cascade of water as it disappeared. When it rose to the surface, a shining fish was grasped in its talons.

"Kak-kak-kak," came a new cry, low and harsh. A great bald eagle soared from a high perch and dove straight at the fish hawk. The eagle swooped at the smaller bird, first over it, then under it in a sudden attack. Their shrieks filled the air as the fish hawk plunged, then climbed with the snowy-headed eagle in close pursuit. Then the fish hawk, carrying the extra weight of the fish, began to tire. Instead of flying, it let the air currents support it. At last, it dropped its fish. It was what the eagle wanted. It dove to catch the fish in its taloned feet before it hit the water, then flapped away with its prize.

Will stamped his foot. "But that wasn't fair," he declared. "That big bird stole the other bird's fish."

Josie was too stunned to reply. Never in her life had she witnessed such a sight. She took Will's hand, and together they watched the fish hawk skim over the water in search of another fish.

"Kyeek! Kyeek! Kyeek!" Down he went again into the water.

This time no eagle flew from above to steal his catch, and he winged away with his fish, leaving the lake suddenly quiet.

Will broke the silence. "I want to go fishing too, Josie," he said.

His matter-of-factness brought Josie up short. "Of course you do," she agreed. She picked up the picnic basket and led the way toward the woods. Now that their bad experiences were all behind them, their day could really begin. "We can walk up Mill Creek, picnic at Silver Thread Falls, and you can fish there." And while Will fished, Josie could read her book. She reached down into the basket just to make sure it was still there.

It was a beautiful hike, only a mile or so. Most of the way they walked up the creek bed, hopping from one huge flat table rock to another. Josie threw away her ruined stockings and carried Will's shoes for him so they were both barefoot. Halfway to the falls, Will slipped on a mossy rock and fell into a shallow pool.

"Now you're wetter than I am." Josie laughed.

The way got steeper as the walls of the ravine, gently sloping at first, soon jutted up a hundred feet on either side of the creek bed. Stubborn pine trees clung to the great cliffs of rock, and the biting fragrance of the needles filled the warm air.

"Look at those fish, Josie. Can I fish here?" Will leaned over a deep pool where baby lake trout circled lazily. The sun dappled the water, throwing golden streaks of light on the fish so they looked almost iridescent.

"Let's keep going, Will," Josie replied. "We should almost be to the falls. I bet they're just around the next bend in the creek."

But they weren't. Nor the bend beyond that. They heard the falls long before they could see them. At each turn in the creek the splashing and gurgling grew louder. Then they saw the falls directly ahead of them, hundreds of rivulets that spilled and bounced down a steep precipice.

"They're gold," Will gasped.

Josie was as astonished as Will. The falls were gold. But how could that be? Josie looked more closely at the water as it splashed down one hundred and sixty feet of what certainly seemed to be rocks of gold. Setting the picnic basket on a high ledge, Josie waded through the stream until she was right beside the falls themselves. The spray was as soaking as a hard rain, but close up, she could see that some kind of yellowish moss grew on the rocks behind the falls. When the sun struck the rocks, the water glittered like gold.

"It's some kind of plant or moss that makes the falls look like gold," Josie called back to Will.

"No, it's gold," he insisted.

Half wanting to believe it herself, Josie didn't contradict him. If they wanted to say the falls were gold, who was there to dispute it?

"We can picnic here, Will, and the two of us can dry out," Josie suggested. She had already picked out a wide rock in the sun. While Will dug into the picnic basket, she spread her skirts as wide as she could and uncoiled her hair so it hung loose on her back to dry. Mrs. Jackman's disapproving expression was still so vivid in her mind, Josie was determined to look respectable when she reboarded the boat. And she wanted to look her best for Cal Evans.

Josie couldn't eat much. The piece of cake had filled her up. But Will ate his way through the cold chicken, sliced corn beef, biscuits and jam, pickles and pickled carrots, and finished up with another slice of cake. When he was done, he wiped the crumbs from his mouth and baited his fishing pole with a worm.

"Will, how old do you guess Mr. Evans is?" Josie asked. It had been on her mind.

"I dunno," Will said as he dropped his line

in a wide pool. "About as old as Papa, I guess."

Josie laughed. "Oh, Will, that mustache just makes him seem older. He's about twenty-two. Or maybe even twenty." His eyes looked young, she thought.

While Will fished, Josie read her book. First she read on her stomach, then on her back, then sitting up. She fluffed out her heavy brown hair. It was almost dry, and so were her clothes. After a while Will put down his pole and snuggled down next to her, resting his head in her lap.

"Your hair looks pretty, Josie," he said sleepily.

Josie had never thought of her hair as pretty. It was brown, and straight. She had always wished it were golden and curly like Will's. Still, it was thick and shiny. Maybe Will was right. Thoughtfully, she twisted it into a thick coil at the nape of her neck and secured it.

"Will, why don't you take a nap?" she suggested. "We still have a long hike to the landing, then the walk all the way from Geneva back to Waterloo." Josie folded the tablecloth to place under Will's head, He was tired and didn't argue. He stretched out on his back with a yawn as Josie picked up her book.

"What's that great big thing up there, Josie?"

Will asked. He sounded half asleep.

Josie followed his line of vision up the ravine wall. There was a puzzling mass of sticks at the top of a tree above the falls. Josie stood up to get a better view but still couldn't figure out what it was. Aroused by Josie's interest, Will stood up, too.

"Maybe it's an Indian house," he said.

"Will, it is *not* an Indian house. It looks more like a nest," she said. But she had never seen such a big nest. She backed off to see better, shielding her eyes from the sun.

It certainly looked like a giant nest. Branches, sticks, reeds, cornstalks, even bones were stacked and intertwined into a castle the size of Mr. Brown's buggy.

"Let's climb up and look. Maybe there's eggs inside," Will pleaded.

"The eggs must have hatched months ago. Still, it would certainly be something to see." Josie couldn't help agreeing. Quickly she scouted the gorge walls. They were steep, but craggy, with lots of crevices. Maybe they could climb up a short distance.

"We'll go up a little way, Will, just to see better," she said. "I'll go first to make sure it's safe." She grabbed a handhold in the rock face. By standing on a fallen log, she was able to pull herself up three feet onto a ledge. She leaned down and took Will's hand and pulled him up beside her.

"Now I'll go up a little farther, then help you," she said, reaching for the next handhold.

"Cheep, cheep, cheep." A plaintive shrill cry whistled above the nest, and a majestic fish hawk was suddenly silhouetted against the sky. With its powerful wings stretched full out, its white breast shone in the sun. As it glided and dipped, Josie realized it was flying closer and closer to the nest. And to them. It must be the fish hawk's nest with young still in it.

"All right, Will, we're getting right down," Josie said firmly. "Me first then you."

Josie stooped down, then half slid, half jumped from her perch. As her feet hit the rocks below, she felt her skirt catch on something, give a hard pull and rip. When she looked back, she saw her dress had snagged on a root. It had torn from the hem to the waist.

"Oh, no," she groaned. She had ruined Mrs. Brown's dress. Even though Mrs. Brown had given it to her, Josie always thought of it as Mrs. Brown's. Her yellow petticoat had ripped, too. She was in tatters.

"Hey, help me down, Josie," Will called

from the ledge. Josie had forgotten all about him. And the fish hawk. She reached up, and Will jumped into her arms. She set him on the rocks and looked at the remains of her dress. She tried to wrap the skirt around her, but it was torn beyond repair.

Will was no help at all. "Mama's gonna be mad. That's her dress," he pointed out.

"What am I going to do?" Josie groaned again. She would just have to get back on the boat with Will, that's what. There was no other way home. But to face all those people again looking even worse than before? She just didn't think she could do it.

A Good Laugh

Josie was worried that she and Will would be late for the afternoon boat, so she hurried him all the way back down Mill Creek. Though she dreaded seeing Cal Evans, she dreaded missing the *Richard Stevens* even more. Will was tired, but she urged him on as they slipped and slid over the mossy creek stones. They arrived in the clearing early. When Josie realized that neither Cal Evans nor the steamboat was in sight, she scurried behind a tall oak tree. Suddenly weak at the thought of the trip ahead of her, she sagged against the tree's rough bark.

Will followed her. "What are you hiding from, Josie?"

"I look awful. And Mr. Evans said he would meet us here. I'd just as soon not see him until I have to," Josie explained. The torn hem of her dress trailed on the ground, showing a great expanse of yellow petticoat. She arranged herself as best she could and waved her skirt to dry the edges. "You keep an eye out for Mr. Evans, Will, but don't go near the dock," she ordered.

Though it was midafternoon, the shadowed woods were damply cool, and the bright moss was spongy under Josie's bare feet. She smelled the sweet fragrance of ferns and pine. Then she heard whistling. Cal Evans had arrived. Josie peeked around the trunk of the tree. Cal was striding into the clearing, swinging a walking stick.

"Wal, young Will, how many fish did you catch, and how was the falls?" Josie heard him ask. "And where's Josie Dexter?"

"I fished and fished, but I didn't catch anything," Will said. "And the falls were nice. They were all real gold."

Cal and Will stood not far from where Josie hid. Cal faced the tree, and when he looked up, Josie was certain he saw her. She ducked back and waited for him to appear. But he surprised her.

"So the fishing was no good. That's too bad, but fishing's like that," Cal said in a loud voice.

"We had a good picnic. Chicken and corned beef and biscuits and pickled carrots and cake," Will chattered on. "Josie didn't eat much. She read a lot. Then she ripped Mama's dress. Mama's gonna be mad."

Josie dug her fingernails into the palms of her hands. If Will said that one more time, she was going to scream.

"Josie ripped her dress?" Cal repeated. "I'm sorry to hear that. Ain't she getting on the boat with us?"

"I don't know," Will answered. "She's over there, hiding behind that tree."

"Seeing as how the *Richard Stevens* is almost here, it'll be an awful long walk home. Or swim, since she's so partial to the water." Cal Evans chuckled.

If the boat were really coming, there was nothing for Josie to do but come out from her hiding place. She picked up the picnic basket and marched out, as if it were perfectly natural to wait for the boat in a stand of oak trees.

"Afternoon." Though she nodded in Cal's direction, she couldn't bring herself to look at him.

"Afternoon, Josie Dexter," Cal replied. "I hear tell from Will that you had a setback on your hike to the falls."

Josie blushed and looked quickly out at the lake. Sure enough, the *Richard Stevens* was steaming toward them. She studied the dark plume of smoke a minute before she answered.

"A-a-as you can see, my skirt got ripped."
If ever in her life she hadn't wanted to stutter,
that moment was it. But wishing wasn't enough.
"It's an em-embarrassment," she added un-
necessarily. Her flaming face and bedraggled
dress told it all.

"I wish't I could help, but I only got the
clothes on my back," Cal said. "Still, didn't
you toss a tablecloth at that goat this morning?
It might tie up into a firstrate apron if you
still got it."

Of course! The tablecloth was folded in the
bottom of the picnic basket with the book.
It was gingham, worn and thin, but presentable,

far more presentable than her dress. She took
it out, shook it, and hurriedly tied it around
her waist. The cloth covered the worst of the
skirt, and if not stylish, it was at least modest.

The boat's whistle blew, sounding even
louder across the stillness of the lake than it
had at the landing in Geneva. Will rushed
out to the wooden dock to watch while Josie
and Cal followed more slowly. With a clang
of the bell, the huge side-wheels trod water,
sending heavy waves shoreward. As the bow
of the big boat swung toward the dock, Will
and Cal positioned themselves in front of Josie
to shield her from view. As soon as the gang-

plank came down, the three of them boarded in a lockstep, first Cal, then Josie, then Will. Josie looked straight ahead, fervently hoping they wouldn't see Mrs. Jackman.

"Most everybody's taking the sun over to port," Cal whispered. "Let's grab us a bench on the starboard side."

Cal's pipe smoke wafted back in Josie's face. "All right," she agreed with a cough.

As they marched toward a bench, a few passengers turned to look. But considering Josie's bare feet, the tablecloth costume, and the strange way the three of them were clumped together, they didn't stir as much interest as Josie had feared.

"That was fun." Will giggled as they found an empty bench. "Let's walk that way again."

"Only if we have to." Josie was relieved the boarding had gone so well.

Though it was still light on the return trip to Geneva, Will slept almost the whole way. His round dirty face was sunburned, and his sailor suit was as grubby as if he had spent the day in the engine room. Josie wondered how she looked. Her black eye was healing, but to a yellowish-purple that was worse, to her mind, than before. At least Cal hadn't asked her about it or even mentioned it.

Josie and Cal slid down to the end of the bench so their talk wouldn't waken Will.

"Tell me about your pipe, Cal. I've never seen one like it," Josie said.

Cal took the pipe from his mouth. "You might say I collect pipes. I went to sea at thirteen. All over the world I been, and at every port I found myself a different pipe. This here is my favorite. A French pipe from Le Havre."

France! Cal had traveled to places Josie had only read about. She looked at him with new respect. "Are you going back to sea?" she asked.

"Six years was enough. I been everywhere and seen everything. Now I'm ready to settle into a local business," Cal said. "I like the nursery work, and Mr. Smith pays me fair."

Josie quickly added the figures. Cal was perhaps nineteen or twenty at the most. That wasn't unreasonably old. And Josie was so tall she looked older than almost fifteen. She was, in fact, as tall as Cal. Maybe taller.

When the final docking whistle blew, they wakened Will and gathered up their belongings. After all the other passengers had got off, they left the *Richard Stevens*. Josie made Cal march in front of her, and Will behind, just like before. As Josie followed Cal, she compared their heights. He was a good inch or two taller than she. Not that it mattered, she assured herself.

"I'll see you and Will home," Cal offered. "My work's done for the day and I like to walk."

"That'd be kind . . . oh, there's Mrs. Jackman." Josie moaned. Mrs. Jackman and her sister were just leaving the boat. The sister was crippled, and the captain was helping her down the gangplank. As Mrs. Jackman followed her sister, she looked right at Josie. Her face was set in tight lines. All of a sudden Josie didn't care. She smiled pleasantly at the two women as they passed her on the jetty. Neither one returned her smile.

Josie wouldn't let it bother her. "Best we get started," she said cheerfully. "Your mama wants you home before dark, Will, and Cal doesn't care to be hiking till midnight."

As she and Will and Cal headed for Waterloo, the sky was just pinkening with the early evening sun. They walked slowly, keeping pace with Will's short strides. A hay wagon passed in the other direction. and the smell of the fresh-mown hay reminded Josie of her mother and the farm. She wondered if her mother had found the dress and bonnet and if she liked them. Her mother had so few pleasures.

As far back as Josie could remember, her mother had never had a fancy-free day all to herself. She had been to quilting bees and cornhuskings but had never spent a day as she pleased such as Josie had just enjoyed.

"That was the best picnic ever, wasn't it?" Will asked, as if he had read her mind.

She took his hand in hers and squeezed it.

"I fancy picnics myself," Cal said. "How about the three of us taking a canalboat up the canal a-ways for a picnic Sunday next?"

"My free day is today," Josie said. "I won't have another till next month."

"Then let's make it next month," Cal said. "And in betwixt mebbe I could come to call."

Josie didn't know what to say. "Well . . ." she began.

Will solved her dilemma. "Yeh, Cal, if you come to call, you and me can play checkers. I can beat my father and Josie too."

Josie laughed, and Cal joined in. Their laughter covered the need for an answer, and they walked on in silence, watching the red ball of a sun fire the sky. High above them, three or four red-tailed hawks soared in circles scouting their evening meal.

Josie pointed them out to Will. "Those are hawks up there."

"Huh, they're small. They're not half as big

as the fish hawk we saw today," Will replied. His voice was scornful.

"I used to like watching the birds at sea," Cal said. "'Course all sailors are partial to albatrosses. They bring a ship good luck."

"Maybe a fish hawk brings good luck too," Will said.

It had better, Josie thought, looking down at her bare feet and ruined dress.

"Josephine! Josephine Dexter!" There was the clatter of horse's hooves and a rattling of a wagon behind them.

Josie didn't even have to turn around. No mistaking that voice. It was Mrs. Abbott. As the old woman reined Rubin to a halt beside them in the road, a cloud of dust swirled up.

"I knew 'twas you, Josephine, even from a distance. You got the broad Dexter shoulders," Mrs. Abbott announced to Josie's dismay. Then Mrs. Abbott blinked. "Why, where in thunder have you been looking like that? And bare feet! You 'pear like you been through a thresher. And what's that wrapped around you, girl, a bedcover?" She burst out with her startling laugh. She threw back her head and slapped her hand on her knee.

It was hard not to join in. Will started to giggle. Then Cal began to chuckle. Even Josie had to laugh. She must really look ridiculous.

Mrs. Abbott was the first to stop. She wiped her eyes. "Wal, girl, I'll give you and your friends a lift if you wants one. I'm going into town to visit Amelia Clark, who's ailing. There's no springs, and not much room, but it beats walking."

Will jumped up front with Mrs. Abbott while Cal and Josie climbed in the back, empty now of milk barrels. Mrs. Abbott clucked to Rubin, and they started off. The little wagon bumped and jarred over the dirt road so that it was hard to talk.

"Sunday next, Josie?" Cal asked as Mrs. Abbott swung off Main Street toward north Williams.

Josie ran her hand over her skirt, trying to straighten it. "I don't know if Mrs. Brown would like that." Josie hesitated. She didn't know about Mrs. Brown. She didn't know about herself either.

Mrs. Abbott reined Rubin up to the Brown's carriage block. "All right, everybody out. I gotta get over to Amelia's," Mrs. Abbott called.

Will scrambled down and darted after the early evening fireflies. Josie and Cal climbed stiffly down from the back.

"Thank you, Mrs. Abbott," Josie called as

the little milk wagon started down the street.

Cal put one foot up on the carriage block and took Josie's hand. He looked her right in the eye. "Sunday next, Josie?" he asked again.

Josie studied his blue eyes a moment, then looked away. "Maybe," she said.

Cal grinned, pulled his pipe from his pocket and stuck it in his mouth. "Farewell, Will," he called. "And I'll see you again, Josie Dexter." He turned on his heel and walked away.

Josie watched him walk down Williams Street until he was swallowed up by the evening gloom. Then suddenly she shivered in the cool dusk. She had almost forgotten Mrs. Brown. Now it was time to face her.

A Parting

Josie opened the gate and followed Will up the front walk. But the pebbles hurt her bare feet, and she hurried ahead of him. She was halfway up the porch steps when she heard the creak, creak of the rocking chair. She peered past the lilac bushes into the gloom. There, on the dark porch, sat Mrs. Brown, silently rocking. Josie was so startled she gasped out loud.

"Will, come here. I want to see for myself if you're all right," Mrs. Brown said quietly. Will hadn't noticed his mother either. But he rushed toward her, his arms out.

"Of course, I'm all right, Mama. Why wouldn't I be?" he cried. "Josie and me had the best picnic ever!"

Mrs. Brown leaned over and gave him a hug. "I'm so glad you're home safe, dear. I've been worried. Now go in the kitchen and eat your supper while I talk to Josie," she ordered. Will ran into the house, slamming the front door behind him.

"Oh, Mrs. Brown, I-I hope we're not late. And I do thank you for giving me the day off, but I feel so bad . . . my . . . your dress got ripped . . ." Josie's tongue tripped over her words.

"Come into the house, Josie," Mrs. Brown interrupted. "I want to take a look at you for myself." Her voice was low and expressionless, and Josie knew she was very angry.

Josie's mouth went so suddenly dry she couldn't answer. She watched the moths beat against the front windows in a frenzy to get at the lighted room inside. The whir of their wings and the soft thud of their bodies against the glass were the only sounds on the porch as Mrs. Brown stood up. With the release of her weight, the empty rocking chair banged on the floor.

Josie followed Mrs. Brown inside, blinking at the unexpected glare of the front hall lamp. As she put the picnic basket down by the umbrella stand, she glanced up. The light reflected off the gold watch Mrs. Brown wore on her full bosom. The time winked at her. Seven thirty.

"Look at you, Josie, just look," Mrs. Brown said. Her voice was flat. "A disgrace, that's what it is. No wonder people are talking."

"I know I look terrible, but it w-w-was an accident. My skirt got caught on a root and ripped. The tablecloth hid the worst of it," Josie explained. She smoothed the cloth across the tear and curled her bare toes up tight as if to hide them.

"I would like you to pack your belongings and leave my house, Josie, right now, before Mr. Brown returns from his meeting," Mrs. Brown said evenly as if she were asking Josie to wash the dishes.

Josie was stunned. "Wh-what do you mean?"

"I mean you're dismissed," Mrs. Brown replied. "It's best you find work elsewhere."

"You're dismissing me because I ripped your dress?" Josie asked.

"It has nothing to do with the dress. I'm dismissing you because of your scandalous behavior today," Mrs. Brown said. Then her face softened. "I'm sorry about this, Josie. If I hadn't seen how you look with my own eyes and hadn't seen that . . . that man with you just now, I wouldn't have believed you were that kind of girl."

"What kind of girl?" Josie demanded, suddenly angry herself.

"The kind of girl that would argue in public with Mr. Hubbard, then, after falling in the lake, shamelessly board the boat in front of a hundred spectators in bare feet and clothes so wet you might as well have had no clothes on at all. And look at you now. In tatters." The words tumbled out. "But for you to pick up with a strange man and go off with him for the day! That was the worst, Josie, the very worst. To disappear all day with a stranger. Who was he? Will might have been in danger and how do you think your behavior looked to others, I ask you? Do you know how many tongues will be wagging by the morrow?"

A moth had flown in the house when the door was opened, and it batted frantically against the lamp. Without knowing she did it, Josie reached up and brushed it to safety. But it flew right back to the light. "But none of that's true . . . I mean, it didn't happen like that. Who told you?" Josie asked.

"My aunt's servant girl heard it at the Cash and Tea Store from Mr. Hubbard, and I heard it in the post office." Mrs. Brown's voice picked up momentum. "And Louise Jackman was just here on her way home from Geneva. She told me how you met that man on the boat and spent the whole day with him. Alone! Do you realize how embarassed I felt? Why, Mrs. Jackman might have thought I had given you my approval." As her voice got lower, her face got redder and redder. Josie knew Mrs. Brown laced her corset too tight, and for a moment thought she might faint. Josie felt dizzy herself.

"But Mr. Evans was kind enough to help me," Josie objected. Under the fury of Mrs. Brown's anger, she had backed up against the banister. "I only met him on the boat. . . ."

Mrs. Brown rolled over Josie's protest as if she hadn't heard it. "Now my friends will have something to talk about besides that Woman's Rights Convention. You." Mrs. Brown's eyes narrowed. "That's it, isn't it? Mary Ann Mc-Clintock has something to do with that convention, doesn't she? And you picked up your outrageous notions at her house yesterday. Troublemakers, that's what those pious Quakers are with their antislavery antics and now this woman's rights nonsense."

Josie pressed hard against the banister. She felt as physically attacked as when Uncle Hiram had struck her. And just as unfairly. She didn't know how to defend herself. She sank down on the second step and looked up at the lamp. The moth was still beating hopelessly against it.

"Mrs. McClintock had nothing to do with what happened today," Josie said. "The ladies were nice as can be and never urged me to do anything but go to their meeting." Josie spoke slowly so she wouldn't stutter. "By any chance, did Mrs. Jackman tell you how I saved Will from a goat?"

"Mama, Josie did save me, she did," Will cried out from the dining room. He ran into the hall and rushed between his mother and Josie. "You're not fair. It was the biggest goat I ever seen, and he would of hurt me bad if Josie hadn't saved me."

"Will, you mustn't eavesdrop. I told you to stay in the kitchen. Now go get some cream from the cellar and finish up the flummery." Mrs. Brown spoke more sharply to Will than Josie had ever heard her.

Though raspberry flummery was Will's favorite desert, he hesitated. "Please don't be mean to Josie, Mama. Please." he begged.

"All right, Josie and I will talk about it," Mrs. Brown said, and Will headed reluctantly for the kitchen.

But Josie didn't want to talk anymore. Mrs. Brown's mind was made up, and what the neighbors thought was more important to her than hearing what really happened. It would be best just to leave without any more argument. Josie turned to go upstairs. Then she remembered Mrs. McClintock's book. She took it from the picnic basket and slipped off its newspaper wrapping. Without thinking, she laid her cheek against the rough leather cover.

"Look at you, Josie. It's unnatural for a girl to have a craving for books," Mrs. Brown said. "Quakers and books do nothing but fill you with radical notions."

Josie started up the stairs without replying.

Her third floor room was under the eaves. After baking in the sun all day, it was still hot. But she was used to its heat, and it never bothered her. Josie looked around. After two years, the small room was just the way she wanted it. Blue and yellow curtains hung at the window, and a blue and yellow rag rug was thrown on the floor. It had taken Josie almost a year to dye and braid the rags to just the right colors. Now she wondered. Was the rug Mrs. Brown's or hers? The rags had been Mrs. Brown's, but the work had been Josie's. She decided to leave it.

She didn't hesitate to take the blue coverlet her grandmother had made. Her initials were woven in the corner and the date, 1808, the year Josie's father had been born. Everything else, the bed, the dresser, the chair, the commode, belonged to the Browns. Quickly, Josie emptied her clothes from the drawers and spread them on the bed. She wouldn't let herself think of where she would go or what she would do. For now, she just wanted to get out of the house.

She took off Mrs. Brown's ruined dress and tossed it over the chair. It took only a moment to slip into her own muslin work dress, her blue stockings, and flat Sunday shoes. She gathered her few possessions together and neatly packed them on the coverlet. Then she folded the coverlet around them and tied the corners in a knot.

Without looking back, Josie left the room and hurried down the stairs. The hall was empty, and Josie was grateful she could leave without having to see Mrs. Brown again.

But Mrs. Brown must have heard her come down the stairs. "Josie, come in here," she called from the dining room. She was seated at the dining-room table, her ample form almost overflowing the narrow chair. Will stood beside her.

"Here's your wages, Josie," Mrs. Brown said, putting two coins on the Turkey red tablecloth. "I hate to see you go like this, but after what happened today, it wouldn't look right for you to stay. Mr. Brown is a moral, upright person, and a banker's business depends on his good reputation."

Such an anger rose in Josie she could almost feel it bubbling inside her. "I'm a moral, upright person too, Mrs. Brown, and I never did anything to disgrace you," she said in a controlled voice.

"Perhaps, Josie, but with everybody talking, it's best you go." Mrs. Brown fingered her watch. Eight twenty, it read. "Still, people do forget, and maybe in five or six months, when all the gossip has died down, you can come back to work for us again."

"Will, did you tell your mother everything that happened today?" Josie asked, though she already knew the answer.

"I told Mama all about the goat and how you saved me and everything," Will said anxiously.

"He told me the best he could," Mrs. Brown said. She put her arm around Will and held him close. "Some of what I said may have come from a misunderstanding, Josie."

"The misunderstanding was that you never asked me for my account. Not once." Josie tried to enunciate each word clearly. "You made up your mind without hearing me out fairly. You were more concerned about what

people might think than what really happened."
Josie remembered Mrs. Stanton had said no
woman could testify in court. This had been
worse. She hadn't been allowed to testify
right here in the house she had called home
for two years. She turned her back and walked
into the front hall.

"Josie!" Will called. He ran after her. "Don't
go, Josie!" Tears ran down his dirty cheeks.

Josie put down her bundle and hugged him.
"It's late, and you're tired, Will. You go on up
to bed," she said.

"But what if I have nightmares, Josie, and
you're not here," he sobbed.

Josie gave him a hard squeeze. "You're a
big boy now, and too old for nightmares, Will.
Why, you're old enough to manage on your
own."

"No, I'm not," he wailed.

Josie stood up quickly and pried his arms
from her skirt. She was almost in tears herself
as she picked up her bundle and went out
into the soft July night. From the house she
heard Will crying and his mother trying to
comfort him. She walked down the porch
steps and smelled the sharp odor of the mari-
golds that bordered the path. She opened the
picket gate and passed quickly through it.

Josie hoped Will could manage on his own. She hoped she could too, but she wondered. All she knew was that she could never go back to the Browns. Not ever.

Advice from Charlotte

Just in case Mrs. Brown was watching, Josie hurried past the hitching post and walked beyond the house. Then she dropped her bundle on the ground and stood for a moment, taking long, deep breaths. Her heart was beating as if she had run a mile.

Now what could she do? Wait until Mr. Brown came home from his meeting? Even if he convinced Mrs. Brown to take her back, Josie would never return. Never! And going to the farm was impossible too. If Uncle Hiram hadn't heard the gossip, he was sure to weasel it out of Josie that she had been dismissed. No, it would be better to wait until she had another job before she saw Uncle Hiram.

Heartsick, Josie looked up and down the familiar street with its row of solid brick houses. Lights twinkled from all the windows. Men sat reading their newspapers while their wives sewed. Across the street old Mr. and Mrs. Wagner sat on their front porch dozing, surrounded by their cats. Next door Mrs. Meeker and her daughter were rolling out pastry dough. Their baking reminded Josie of Charlotte. That's where she would go. Charlotte would take her in.

Charlotte lived with her family just over the Seneca River in Fayette. With her bundle of belongings slung over her shoulder, Josie started out at a trot. She couldn't get there fast enough. Wild thoughts raced through her mind as she ran over the bridge. What if Charlotte weren't home? Or if she wouldn't take Josie in?

By the time Josie reached Charlotte's street she was so winded she had to slow to a walk. Only a few of the small, run-down houses were lighted, and the night was dark. The moon was shaded by clouds, and only a few stars shone. The beautiful sunset had staged a turnabout. Just like my beautiful day, Josie thought.

She made her way to Charlotte's back yard and peeked in the kitchen window. Charlotte was washing her hair over a tin basin. Her mother and her sister, Emma, were seated at a table sewing. But Josie wanted to see Charlotte alone. She sat down on the back-porch step to wait. As she waited, her sense of panic eased. Charlotte *was* home. Charlotte *would* take her in.

As Josie sat staring into the shadowed night, a basinful of soapy water sailed past her.

"Hey!" she shouted.

"Who's there?" Charlotte called out. Because the kitchen light was behind her, Josie couldn't see Charlotte's face. But her compact, wiry body was silhouetted in the doorway.

"It's me, Josie," Josie answered. She stepped onto the porch.

Charlotte squinted into the darkness. "What are you doing here?"

"Oh, Charlotte, the worst thing happened to me today — " Josie began.

"So the story was true." Charlotte interrupted with a laugh as she rubbed her wet hair with a big cloth. "When I heard you were running around a boat half naked, then going off with some mysterious man, I didn't believe it. I said you'd never do such a daring thing." She sounded amused, and a sense of relief flooded Josie. After all, she hadn't done anything so wrong.

"I was not half naked. I was wet, I'll admit, but I had all my clothes on. And the man wasn't mysterious at all. He was just being helpful," Josie replied. "Still, people are talking, and Mrs. Brown dismissed me because of the gossip."

Charlotte stopped rubbing her head. "She didn't!" she exclaimed indignantly.

"Just like that." Josie snapped her fingers.

"After all you've done for the Browns?" Charlotte's voice rose. "Well, good riddance to them, I'd say." She paused. "But you'll miss Will, won't you?" she added gently.

Oh, how Josie would miss Will. But she didn't want to think about Will right now. "Can I spend the night with you, Charlotte?" she asked instead.

Charlotte looked back at the house. From inside came the sounds of a baby crying, boys' voices raised in argument, and the old grandmother shouting at them. It was a small and very crowded house.

Charlotte wound the cloth around her head and knotted it. "Lucy's gone for the night, so there's room in the bed with Emma and me," she said. "Even three to a bed is better than the farm, isn't it?"

Charlotte and Josie looked at each other as thoughts of Hiram Dexter passed wordlessly between them. Josie nodded. By now she was so tired she could have slept on the floor.

Charlotte led the way through the kitchen. After a few words of explanation to her mother and Emma, they climbed the stairs to Charlotte's room. Even with the door closed, they could hear the boys scrapping and the grandmother yelling at them to be still.

"Charlotte, I hate to ask you, but I haven't eaten since noon. Do you think I could have a cup of tea?" Josie asked.

"Wait here, and I'll get us some tea and gooseberry pie I brought home from the bakery today," Charlotte said.

After Charlotte left, Josie sank down on the bed. She eased off her tight Sunday shoes and looked around the room. The wide double bed took up most of the space, with two dressers jammed against one wall and a cupboard by the window. The only light came from a couple of tallow candles. A small bedside table was crammed with books, needlework, magazines. And cutout leather gloves. Surprised, Josie picked one up.

"Charlotte, are you a stitcher?" she asked when Charlotte returned with a tray.

Many women stitched leather gloves at night to earn spare money. The leather pieces came from the factories at Gloversville to be hand-stitched at home, then returned. But the square-pointed needle was awkward to use, and the heavy linen thread had to be constantly waxed. It took real skill to produce a neat, close-fitting glove, and it was a hard way to earn pennies.

"It was Pa's idea," Charlotte admitted as she poured the steaming tea. Her voice was sheepish, and Josie knew her friend was embarrassed. "But he lets us girls keep half the wages, and I'm going to need every cent if I want to learn to be a typesetter." As if in defiance, she picked up a nearly finished glove and began to work on it.

"A typesetter!" Josie exclaimed. A woman wanting to be a typesetter? It was as farfetched as wanting to be a sea captain.

"Why not? There's no law that says I can't," Charlotte retorted. "The trouble with you, Josie, is you don't know what or who you want to be. For instance, what are you going to do now, be an operative at the woolen mill?" Charlotte's tone was caustic. A pallid-looking lot, the mill girls were cooped up in the factory from dawn until dark, their lives regulated by the mill bell. Charlotte knew how Josie felt about mill work. Still, there weren't many choices open to her.

"I guess I'll hire out to some other family in town," Josie said with a shrug as if she didn't care. She sipped the hot tea.

Charlotte finished the glove, then sat on it so the heat of her body would straighten the leather. "There, that's what I mean," she said. "Whatever happens to you just happens. Can't you get fired up about anything or have some ambition? Why, I'm earning and saving and learning all the time. I've even been to the Seneca County *Courier* office to watch them set type."

Charlotte always amazed Josie. "You don't want to get married?" she asked. For some silly reason, Cal Evans popped into her mind. She wondered if she would ever see him again.

"Oh, someday, but not until I've done the things I want to do for myself," Charlotte answered quickly as if she had long ago made that decision. She picked up another glove to work on.

The house was quiet. The boys must have fallen asleep, and the old grandmother too. Josie could hear the night noises from outside and smell the spicy fragrance of Mrs. Woodward's herb garden, summer savory, thyme, mint, tarragon, all in season and ready for cutting. In the room the tallow candles didn't shed much light, and Charlotte had to hold the work close to her eyes. Josie slowly finished her pie as she watched Charlotte sew.

"Uncle Hiram said I was a thief. Mrs. Abbott told me I was like uncooked dough. Today a young man said I was spunky. Mrs. Brown called me a disgrace. Now you say I have no ambition. It gets me to wondering who I am and what I'm good for." Josie spoke carefully. Usually she was at ease with Charlotte and didn't stutter, but she wasn't used to talking about herself.

She thought Charlotte would jump in with an opinion as usual, but Charlotte surprised her. "Sometimes you can be a lot of different people until you decide once and for all what you want to make of yourself. And that's something you have to do on your own."

It seemed like a vast undertaking. There wasn't anything Josie could do especially well. Bake, sew, garden, cross-stitch. She wasn't very good at any of them. She liked children, and they liked her. But teach? She had hardly been to school herself.

"There's nary a thing I can think of, Charlotte," Josie said, and she felt more discouraged than ever. Charlotte was so clever and capable she didn't just undertake a project, she attacked it.

Charlotte laughed. "I didn't expect an answer right off. You're not fifteen yet, and there's time to think about it. Just don't push it to the back of your mind forever." She picked up a book from the table. A newspaper clipping stuck out from one of its pages, and Josie knew right away what it was.

"Come with us to the rights convention," Charlotte said, handing Josie the paper. "I'm working at the bakery tomorrow night and Friday night, so I can have the time off. All the O'Hara girls are going, and so is Sarah Post, and you know what a dragon her mother is. It will open up ideas for all of us."

Didn't Charlotte understand? Josie couldn't give up two days to a convention when she didn't have a job. With Lucy coming back tomorrow, she didn't even have a bed to sleep in. But to please Charlotte, Josie took the newspaper and made a pretense of reading it.

The bedroom door flew open, and Emma sailed into the room. "I had no idea it was so late. It's near eleven o'clock," she declared. "With us due at the bakery at four, Charlotte, we shoulda been asleep hours ago."

Emma's arrival saved Josie from having to answer Charlotte, but their conversation stuck in her mind. As they slipped out of their dresses and into their nightclothes, Josie couldn't help envying Charlotte her determination. Charlotte was so sure this convention would provide answers to her questions. And maybe it would.

But for the time being Josie couldn't afford the luxury of having such hopes for herself. All that mattered now was finding work and a place to live.

Rainy Tuesday

Charlotte and Emma rose before dawn. Though the sisters tried to be quiet, they woke Josie as they rolled out of bed. Not accustomed to sleeping three in a bed, Josie had spent a restless night, and now that it was time to get up, she could have slept forever. Especially when she heard the tip-tap of rain on the roof. She lay still and listened to the muffled confusion of Charlotte and Emma dressing. Then they tiptoed out to the privy.

In one sense, the sound of rain was satisfying. Since Josie hadn't done the Monday wash as usual, she had planned to do it today. Maybe by the time Mrs. Brown had done all the wash herself and hung it up indoors she'd wish she hadn't been so hasty. Josie sighed. She was a dreamer. All the rain really meant was that she would have to wear her good Sunday shawl to keep dry. Rain or no rain, she had to look for work today.

Charlotte stuck her head in the door and waved. "Bye, Josie, we're off. Now don't forget. When you find a job, tell them you won't commence til after the convention, hear?"

Josie had to laugh. Charlotte would never give up. "Good-bye," she called. Then she sat straight up in bed. Charlotte's mention of the convention made her think of Mrs. McClintock. Mrs. McClintock was sure to know of families in town who might need help. It at least gave Josie a place to start, and she could return Mrs. McClintock's book as an excuse to see her.

Feeling better about her prospects, Josie got out of bed and dressed. With hard strokes, she brushed out her thick hair and knotted it tight. And neat. Above all, she wanted to look neat and reliable. If only her black eye were healed. She held the looking glass up to the window. Her eye was still discolored, but face powder would hide the worst of it. She rummaged through Charlotte's cluttered dresser top until she found a box of orrisroot powder. She rubbed some on. There, it did look better.

Quickly Josie tidied the room and tucked her bundle of belongings under the bed, knowing that Charlotte wouldn't mind. Shadings of gray had lightened the window by the time she made her way down the narrow stairs. But as she started out, it seemed to be raining harder than ever.

Mrs. McClintock answered Josie's knock

promptly. "Why, Josie, come in out of the wet," she said with a smile.

"I came to return your book. And to see you," Josie explained. She cleaned her muddy shoes on the boot scraper and shook out her soggy shawl before she stepped into Mrs. McClintock's tidy kitchen. Newly tied herbs hung from the ceiling rafters to dry, and a cheerful bowl of yellow bachelor buttons brightened the kitchen table. It was a welcoming room, and all of a sudden Josie ached to be a part of it.

"Mrs. McClintock, do you need help, a hired girl like me to work for you?" she asked.

Mrs. McClintock looked at Josie with thoughtful eyes. "Thou is no longer working for Rhoda Brown?" she asked.

Josie fingered the book in her hand, then laid it on the table. "No, Mrs. Brown heard . . . certain stories . . . and dismissed me." Perhaps Mrs. McClintock had heard the stories too.

She had. "A small village like Waterloo enjoys its gossip. Thou knows all the furor the rights convention has stirred up." Mrs. McClintock's laugh was rueful. "Everyone's excited for a few days. Then something new distracts them. I know thee to be a decent girl, Josie, and thou must ignore it."

Josie was so touched that when she tried to express her thanks, her smile trembled. Neither Mrs. Brown nor Mrs. McClintock had asked her what really happened. The difference was, Mrs. McClintock trusted her and didn't care what people thought.

"If you're willing to have me, I'd hire out for free," Josie pleaded. If only she could. . . .

But Mrs. McClintock shook her head. "Now that my girls are older, Josie, there isn't enough to keep even one person busy. Much as I would like thee here," she added.

Josie knew the idea had been too good to come true. "Do you know any family who might need me?" she asked more practically.

"Let me think," Mrs. McClintock said as she walked to the kitchen window and looked out. The day was as gray as her Quaker dress, and a steady rain still wept down the glass. Absentmindedly Mrs. McClintock took a cloth and wiped the window. Her calico cat rubbed against her skirts, her tail straight up, a deep thrum purring in her throat. "Well, there's the Ames," Mrs. McClintock finally said. "Kate Ames' parents live with her, and they've gotten very feeble."

Of course. Josie should have thought of them. Miss Ames' father was blind, and her mother had such a wandering mind she roamed about town, forgetting where she lived and even what her name was. Josie had taken the old lady home one day herself.

"That's just the place," Josie replied, wrapping her damp shawl about her head. As she reached for the door, Mrs. McClintock touched her arm.

"Thou should know, Josie, that Miss Ames is a little...." Mrs. McClintock hesitated. "Well, she's fussier than most, and it might not work out. If it doesn't, thou can try the Kerrs over to Walnut Street. Mrs. Kerr just had her seventh baby, and she's without help. And, Josie, do think about coming to our convention on the morrow. I'm sure thou would be interested in what we have to say."

"I'll try, Mrs. McClintock, I promise," Josie replied. And she meant it. If going to the convention would repay Mrs. McClintock for her trust, maybe Josie would try to go.

She ran all the way to Miss Ames' house east of town. It was a handsome house, but run-down. All the shutters needed rehanging, but Josie was sure she could fix them, and the knowledge gave her confidence.

But Miss Ames didn't even ask her in the kitchen. Josie stood huddled under the overhang of the back door, trying to avoid a stream of water that poured from a gutter into the rain barrel. From inside she could hear Miss Ames' mother. "Kate, I want my tea. Where's my tea?" Josie found it difficult to explain what she was there for.

"I'm looking for work, Miss Ames, and thought perhaps you needed help," she began. "I'm strong and able."

"It seems to me, Josephine, you don't show very good judgment," Miss Ames said, her thin black eyebrows scowling. Her beautiful raven hair was parted in the middle and pulled into a knot. No side curls softened her heart-shaped face. "Don't you know Louise Jackman lives right next door?" she asked. "She was over this morning and told me everything that happened yesterday. The good Lord knows I do need help, but not that badly. I grew up with your uncle, and by all that's holy, you two are cut from the same cloth. No, Josephine, you'll find no work here. Good-bye," she said, and firmly closed the door.

Though the word "but" was on Josie's lips, she never had the chance to get it out. Her anger almost choked her. Miss Ames, of all people, had no right to act virtuous. She had lived for years with a paint salesman, and there wasn't a soul in town who didn't know it. Every time the man came to Waterloo he stayed at her house. Then he had married and never returned. And yet Miss Ames had looked down on Josie! Furious, Josie aimed a mighty kick at Miss Ames' back door. Though her toes curled up with pain, it made her feel better. Miss Ames was probably right about Josie and her uncle being alike. Josie was sure he would have done the same thing.

Cutting straight across Miss Ames' front lawn, Josie ran down the muddy street. The faster she was away from that place, the better. The street was silent as she headed back toward town. There were no children playing or even the usual dogs. There was just the steady slap of rain on the broad-leafed maple trees that bordered the street. Josie's shoes and stockings were soaked, and the hem of her skirt was ringed with mud. Without warning, a horse and buggy drove by, throwing up a spray of dirty water that soaked her dress. It was too much.

"You . . . you . . ." Josie spluttered. Then she pushed the wet hair back from her face and shook out her skirts. She would not be bested. Miss Ames wasn't the only apple in the barrel. She would try the Kerrs.

Mrs. Kerr answered the door with a new baby in her arms and a toddler hanging onto her apron. As soon as Josie gave her name and asked for work, Mrs. Kerr eagerly invited her in the kitchen. Another child was barricaded behind a ring of chairs, and three boys were on the floor playing with a set of toy soldiers. The kitchen was a sight. A basketful of soiled diapers was shoved under a table, and a pile of dirty dishes filled the sink. A pot of mush had boiled over on the stove, and the scorched smell filled the room. A hissing teakettle steamed furiously.

"How did you know I needed help?" Mrs. Kerr asked. A wide smile brightened her tired face. "I've had one girl after another leave . . . not that they don't like it here, of course, but it's just they can make more money at the mill. I only pay sixty cents a week, Josephine, but we have a spare bed that you can have all to yourself. If you want, you can start right now," she said hopefully.

The baby had begun to cry, and Josie could see a fight building among the boys on the floor. She took off her shawl and laid it over a chair to dry. She hardly knew where to begin. It didn't matter. She was hired, and by someone who was thrilled to have her.

"Josephine Dexter, this is my husband," Mrs. Kerr said, waving to a heavyset man who had entered the kitchen. Josie recognized him as a clerk at Allen's Boot and Shoe Store. "Josephine is our new hired girl," Mrs. Kerr explained. "Aren't we lucky?"

Josie smiled at the man and started to clean the stove.

"You're Hiram Dexter's daughter?" Mr. Kerr asked.

Josie turned around. "Stepdaughter," she corrected.

"You been working over to the Browns' on Williams Street?" he asked.

"For t-t-two years," Josie stammered, suddenly cautious.

"And they discharged you?" he demanded.

"Ah, well . . . yes," she admitted.

"Nancy, come out in the hall so's we can talk." Mr. Kerr signaled his wife. With a puzzled expression, she followed him, the crying baby still on her hip.

They were gone only a few minutes. Josie halfheartedly finished cleaning the stove. Even before Mrs. Kerr came back, Josie knew the verdict.

"I'm sorry, Josephine, but right now, we don't really need help . . . at least for the summer. Maybe in the fall, but . . . well, I'm so sorry," she apologized. She looked distressed.

Josie had already picked up her shawl. "That's all right, Mrs. Kerr, I understand," she said as she shook out the wet shawl and tied it over her head. Though it didn't make it any easier, Josie did understand. She felt numb with disappointment as she walked out of the house. It was still pouring, but she hardly noticed.

Josie was sure of only one thing. Never again would she humiliate herself by asking for hired girl work in this town. But work was what she needed. And today. It left one other choice open to her. The woolen mill.

Mill Girl

Josie stood in the rain and looked across the raceway at the Waterloo Woolen Manufacturing Company, a dreary cluster of limestone buildings on the Seneca River. Josie studied the bell tower on the west mill. Over the years she had heard the bell so often she hardly noticed it. Report-for-work bell rang at six, with the dismissal bell tolling at dusk. For the first time, Josie realized what the bell must mean to the mill workers.

"Out of me way, gal." She heard a shout behind her. She jumped back just in time to avoid being splashed by a horse-drawn wagon full of sheep wool. An oilskin was pulled over the wool, and the driver was huddled under a black umbrella. He clattered over the narrow bridge that spanned the raceway.

As Josie followed the wagon across the bridge she saw that the mill was really an island. Part of the Seneca River had been diverted to form a raceway. The raceway ran in front of the property, and the Seneca and Cayuga

Canal flowed behind it. Josie guessed that the water pouring under the mill from the raceway to the canal provided the mill's power. She felt like Sir Walter Scott's Lady Rowena about to cross a moat into the enemy castle. When the drawbridge pulled up, she would be prisoner.

She snapped her shawl impatiently around her shoulders. She was being silly. Probably the mill was full of workers who were satisfied with their jobs and happy with their wages. But it was hard for Josie to shake her dark mood. Maybe it was the beating rain. Or maybe it was the drab gray buildings. Grass and young trees had once been planted but had long since been trampled. The geraniums and day lilies that bordered the buildings had been beaten flat by the rain.

As Josie made her way through the mud toward the west mill, a dull, buzzing sound hummed in the air. The closer she came to the building, the louder it grew. With each step her feet slopped in her sodden shoes. She tried to scrape them clean at the mill's entrance, but it was hopeless. She pulled open the wide door. As she entered the main hall, she was bombarded by a roar of sound. The whir of massive belts and drums made her ears hurt and her insides quiver. She tried to hide her fright as she approached a man standing near the door.

"I'm looking to apply for work," she shouted at him.

"You want to be an operative?"

At Josie's nod, the man jerked his thumb over his shoulder at a flight of stairs. Josie lifted her drenched skirts and started up them. But when she opened the door at the top, it was if she had released all the demons of Hades. It wasn't just the clatter and whirl of the machinery that startled her. It was the thick choking air as well. Dumbfounded, Josie stared into a huge loft room. Women and children tended the wheeling, rattling machines as calmly as if they were on a Sunday stroll.

Someone pushed rudely past her. She was blocking the doorway. She had either to leave or to go in. How tempting it was to run back down the stairs and out into the cool, fresh rain. Instead, she headed for a wide desk set back against the loft-room wall. A man sat at the desk, a quill behind his ear. He was running his finger down a column of figures.

"Pardon me, sir," Josie yelled at him. He didn't look up.

"Good afternoon, sir," she shouted louder,

and this time caught his attention. "I'm looking for work as an . . . an . . . operative," she explained. It was hard to get the strange word out.

"Yeah?" The man raised thick gray eyebrows. "Yesterday one of my girls in the spinning room quit, and I ain't replaced her yet. I guess you can have a try at it, if'n you want to start work today."

Josie needed the job, but now that it was hers she wanted to run from it. She sneezed and brushed what felt like greasy cobwebs from her face.

"I can start right off," she shouted, "but I'll need a place to live."

"You ain't a local?" the man asked.

Josie played deaf. "I need a bed somewheres."

The man shrugged his shoulders. "The operative that quit lived over to Mrs. Henry's boardinghouse in town. I reckon you can take her place. At suppertime tell Mrs. Henry you want to board there. You got half an hour for meals, three times a day. Wages is a dollar a week, with us paying a dollar fifteen for your board. Sundays, Thanksgiving, and fastdays you're free. Onc't you're hired official, you can sign our rules and regulations, but for now, I'll show you where you work." He hadn't asked Josie's name. Or given his. It didn't seem to matter, at least to him.

Holding her wet skirts tight, Josie followed the man the length of the room past gigantic machinery. Everything seemed to move at different speeds. Great drums whirled near the ceiling. Chattering belts and pulleys zigzagged in every direction. Turning rollers rigged with hundreds of pins cleaned and pulled wide strings of greasy wool.

"Carding machines," the man barked, leading Josie through a far door into another whitewashed loft room. In this room, hundreds of spindles whirled on long frames. Each spindle held a bobbin that fed a thick strand of wool onto another bobbin on a lower frame. The dizzying speed of the spindles made Josie lightheaded. She leaned against the doorframe and watched young girls run around the whirring machinery replacing bobbins as they emptied. This must be the spinning room. But how could Josie ever do that?

"This is where you work, and these here are jenny frames. Your foreman ain't here now, but one of the girls can show you what to do," the man said. "It's the easiest work in the mill, and there's no trick to learning it. Just take off the full bobbins, and put them on the cart for the weaving room. Put the empty bobbins on the cart for the carding room, and they'll be returned ready for spinning." He turned on his heel and went back through the carding room.

Two girls who looked a little older than Josie stood by a long bench under the windows. As soon as the man left the room, they promptly sat down and stared at Josie. The other girls seemed much younger. They looked familiar but she didn't know them. No one spoke as Josie hung her shawl on a wall peg. The air in the loft was so hot and sticky, Josie was sure neither the shawl nor she would ever dry. She was sure her ears would never recover either.

Backing up against the wall, Josie stood by the long bench to watch the operatives do their work. But the two girls on the bench were a distraction. They sat with their heads together, gesturing and giggling. Though Josie couldn't hear a word they said, she was sure they were talking about her. She tried to smooth down her wet skirts and tuck in loose strands of hair. All the other girls wore aprons, and she wished she had thought to bring hers.

One of the girls on the bench was plump and curly-headed. The other was thin with such almond-shaped eyes she looked almost

Oriental. Both girls were startlingly pale. In fact, all the girls in the room were pale. By mid-July Josie found it hard *not* to have a suntan.

At the thought of the sun, Josie looked out the window behind her. But she couldn't see anything more than the roofs of the bleak mill buildings. Not a treetop or even a bird was in sight. Only the gray rain beating down. It was strange to see the rain and not be able to hear it. Josie reached up her hand as if to feel its wetness through the glass.

"Are the windows always closed?" she shouted at the curly-headed girl.

"Of course. They're nailed shut. The humider, the better," the girl replied. "If the windows are open, the wind might break the yarns or dry them out." Then she turned to her friend, and they giggled at such a stupid question.

If the girls were going to be so unfriendly, Josie wouldn't ask them anything more. Instead she watched the other workers and tried to remember what the man had told her. She understood what needed to be done, but to stick her hands in and out of those whirling spindles terrified her.

Josie circled around the jenny frame with its rolling pulleys and spinning bobbins as if

it were a wild horse. There she spotted a
bobbin that was almost full, with the one
above it nearly empty. Snap. The empty bobbin
clattered around and around. For a moment,
Josie paused, then saw her own hand reach
in and yank off the empty bobbin. She was
hardly aware she had done it. Before she could
let herself think, she quickly grabbed the full
bobbin. But her hand was unsteady, and she
dropped it on the floor. In horror, she watched
the bobbin roll under the frame, the colorless
yarn unwinding as it curved out of sight.

Josie dropped to her hands and knees and
peered under the whirring machines. There

was nothing to see but dust. Carefully, oh, so carefully, she slipped her open hand under the groaning, moving belts and gingerly felt around for the bobbin. Farther and farther in she reached until she was lying flat on her stomach with her arm straight out under the machinery. There, the tips of her fingers had it. But as she touched the bobbin, it rolled away from her. With her arm outstretched as far as it would go, she was able to grasp the edge of the bobbin with her fingers and gently ease it out.

As Josie scrambled to her feet, she brushed off the bobbin and wound up the yarn. Though her still-damp dress was coated with wool and lint, at least she hadn't lost her arm at the elbow. But when she glanced toward the bench, the two girls were laughing so hard they were almost doubled over.

Feeling herself blush, Josie placed the bobbin on the weaving room cart. Now she was determined to do it right. When the next bobbin filled, she stepped up to it and firmly lifted it from the frame. Then she removed the empty bobbin boldly. After that, it was easier.

The younger girls chatted and talked among themselves. Three of them even played a game of jacks on the floor. But Josie stayed with the bobbins as if her life depended on them. It wasn't until the supper bell tolled that she realized how her head throbbed. And how hungry she was. She had been minding the machines so intently her muscles ached. And she had only been working five hours. It seemed like ten. When the machinery slowed and stopped, she heard a shrill, sustained ringing. She wasn't sure if it were the machines or her own ears.

At the tolling of the bell the girls ran for the door, snatching their cloaks from the pegs as they fled. From the far room, Josie could hear the stampede of feet pounding down the stairs. Doors slammed. Voices called back and forth as if the girls wanted to make sure they could still talk. And hear. Josie was the last to leave the room. She took down her shawl from the peg and walked through the silent carding room. The bushy-browed man was still at his desk, the quill now in his hand as he checked out his workers. He looked up at Josie.

"Say, ain't you the new operative? I forgot to get your name and the other information," he said. His quill was poised over his ledger-book.

Josie looked back at the rows of silent machinery. The girls ahead of her sounded like cackling geese. To work here was to be like an empty bobbin, endlessly spinning. And to be pale as undyed wool.

"I'll give it to you later," she replied as she stepped past his desk and started down the stairs. "Maybe," she added softly to herself.

Homesick

By the time Josie crossed the bridge over the raceway most of the girls had scattered. Not girls, Josie corrected herself, operatives. It was a descriptive word. An operative wasn't a person at all. She was just part of the operation.

The rain had almost stopped, and Josie carried her wet shawl rather than wear it. Her skin itched from the tiny particles of wool that clung to her. Even her throat was scratchy, and the sour smell of wet wool was gagging. As Josie headed for the road, she looked at the dark buildings and shuddered.

A robin hopped across her path. It stopped and tugged at a long worm. As Josie watched the robin fly away with its prize, she suddenly longed for the farm. The day had been so dreadful, so humiliating. She just couldn't face a boardinghouse full of strangers. All she wanted was to go home, to see her mother and the boys. She wanted to be part of the family. She wanted to be reassured that she was needed and of worth.

And, after all, she could be a help on the farm. With the haying to finish up, it was the busiest season of all. There was always weeding to be done, and repairs to be made around the property. But Josie knew those weren't her real reasons. What she wanted right now was to see her mother. As for Uncle Hiram, she would face him when the time came.

Josie decided to swing down past Charlotte's house and pick up her belongings before she started home. But as she set out for town, it was as if her feet had a will of their own. Instead of heading toward Charlotte's, she turned north toward Williams Street. The Browns lived only a few blocks from the mill. All day Josie had been able to push thoughts of Will to the back of her mind, but before going home, she just had to see him.

By now Will should have finished his supper and, with luck, might be in the carriage house playing with the cats. Running into Mrs. Brown was the last thing Josie wanted, so she approached the house from the rear. She ducked through the door of the carriage house, where the pungent odor of hay, horse, and leather greeted her.

"Will, are you in here? It's me, Josie," she

called softly. The cats stretched and walked away. The horse shuffled in his stall, but no one answered. Josie pushed an empty box to the far wall and climbed up to peek out the window. There was Will in the back yard, leaning over his rabbit cage, feeding cabbage leaves to his rabbit. Josie tapped on the window.

Startled, Will looked around. Then his face broke into a huge grin. Josie met him halfway as he ran around to the carriage house door. She braced herself for the full force of his hug.

"Josie, you're back! I knew you'd come," he cried.

"Will, I only came to see how you're doing," Josie explained. She took both his hands in hers.

He stopped short and looked at her with accusing blue eyes. "But I had a nightmare. I dreamed that a big goat butted me right off the roof of our house. I told you I'd have a nightmare, and I did." Then he smiled. "But now you're back, I won't have any more."

Josie shook her head in mock despair. "You just talk yourself into nightmares. Will. Promise to try something for me?"

He nodded, his face serious.

"Promise you won't eat anything after supper." Josie said. "And promise you won't even think about nightmares again. When you go to bed, you think of our nice waterfall, all gold and sparkly."

"But you'll be here, won't you, Josie?" he asked. He looked worried.

"No, I'm going home," Josie said. "I have a mother too, and she needs me just like your mother needs you." Or vice versa, she amended silently as she hugged Will good-bye. His solid little body was so dear and his arms around her neck were so binding it was hard to pull away. "I'll be back, Will. Count on it."

"Can you come see me on Sunday?" he asked. His arms were still tight around her neck.

"I'm not sure about Sunday, but when I come I'll try to bring Sam and Robert with me." Will's mention of Sunday reminded Josie of Cal. "Will, if Cal Evans comes to see me on Sunday next, can you tell him I've gone home to my farm? The Dexter farm, northwest of town. Can you remember that?" she asked.

He nodded. "Me and Cal are gonna play checkers," he bragged.

It was a good time to leave. "Good-bye, Will," Josie said. She pulled away and hurried from the carriage house. When she looked back, Will was holding one of his cats and waving to her. She felt better. Will would be all right.

Though the rain had stopped, by the time

Josie reached Charlotte's house she was soaked. Her mud-caked skirts were a dead weight around her ankles, and her shoes were so wet the leather had stretched all out of shape. It was still a long walk to the farm, and Josie counted on being in and out of the Woodwards' house quickly. To her dismay, it was Charlotte who opened the door.

"Charlotte, I thought you were due back at the bakery tonight," she said, hoping against hope that Charlotte wouldn't demand a report of her day. She stepped into the kitchen. When she smelled mutton cooking, her hunger returned with a rush.

"I'm going later," Charlotte replied. "But what about you? Did you find work? When do you start, and can you get the morrow free?" she asked. Her brown eyes were intense.

"I promise someday to tell you the whole story. But not now. Please not now, Charlotte, I'm going home to the farm and I'd like to pick up my things and be off," Josie said. Her voice was weary.

"Of course, Josie, but why — " Without waiting to hear the rest, Josie walked past Charlotte into the hall. She tiptoed by the front room, where the Woodward family had gathered, and up the narrow stairs to Charlotte's bedroom. When she returned to the kitchen with her belongings, Charlotte was by the stove.

"I thank you, Charlotte. And don't worry about your book. I'll get it to you soon," Josie said. She was anxious to leave before Charlotte could protest her return to the farm.

But Charlotte never said a word. As Josie started for the door, Charlotte shoved a napkin-wrapped bundle in her hand. It was warm and smelled delicious. She had a wry smile on her face as if to say she knew Josie better than Josie knew herself.

Josie smiled back. "You're capital," she said. With both hands full, she gave Charlotte an awkward hug.

The package held a mutton chop, half a loaf of bread, and a wedge of cheese. As Josie walked toward the farm, she dug into it. The food gave her a real lift. It wasn't just that it tasted so good or even that Charlotte had thought to pack it. It was that Charlotte had done it without stopping her with a hundred questions. And Josie knew what an effort that had been.

The rain still hung and dripped from the trees, and the road was a soupy mire. By now Josie didn't care. She cut across fields and pastures, the tall grass soaking her dress to the knees. After the rain, the mosquitoes were out in full force, swarming in such numbers, Josie could hear their buzzing. The swallows, in turn, were out in pursuit of the insects. They couldn't eat enough of the pesky mosquitoes to suit Josie. She was covered with bites.

When she reached Mrs. Abbott's property, Josie cut through the back pasture. The grazing cows looked up as she headed toward the woods that separated the two farms.

"Josephine, is that you?" Josie heard Mrs. Abbott call from the far side of the pasture. Dusk had begun to settle, and Mrs. Abbott was so shaded by a wide chestnut tree Josie hadn't noticed her.

"Aye, Mrs Abbott, it's just me, going home," Josie replied. How good those words sounded.

Mrs. Abbott walked toward her, a saw in her hand. "'Pears to me you spend more time out here than you do in town. Guess that Hiram Dexter's such a jim-dandy you can't resist him," she teased. She elbowed Josie's arm as she laughed at her own wit.

"You're right. Uncle Hiram's my favorite uncle," Josie joked in turn, though she didn't even want to think of Hiram Dexter.

"Say, I saw your ma last week and told her about the dress you made her. She was real pleased." Mrs. Abbott hiked up her skirt and rested one booted foot on a tree stump as if settling in for a chat. Despite her impatience, Josie noticed that Mrs. Abbott wore neither petticoats nor stockings. Tired of dragging around the sodden weight of her own skirts, it seemed a sensible idea.

"Your ma wasn't much int'rested in the meeting on the morrow," Mrs. Abbott continued. "How about you, Josephine?" You decided yet?"

"Well, I don't know," Josie answered. She still had to make up her mind about the mill job.

"If you want to go with me, be here afore five. I aim to deliver my milk in Waterloo early, then leave for Seneca Falls," Mrs. Abbott said as one of her cows ambled up behind her and nudged her arm.

"I'll come before five if I decide to go." Josie left it open. That way the mill job was still a possibility, and she hadn't broken her promise to Mrs. McClintock.

Mrs. Abbott took a cake of salt from her apron pocket and laid it on her open palm. "Here, Daisy," she said absentmindedly. The cow licked the salt from her hand. "Daisy's not letting down much milk lately, and I don't know what ails her," Mrs. Abbott said. Her bright blue eyes turned serious. "I just ain't got the vim to tend the cows proper. Even sawing down that old limb's a chore. Wal, Josephine, you don't want to hear my tales of woe. Run along and try to get back in the morning, hear?"

As Josie turned to go, Mrs. Abbott held up her hand. "If you go through them woods, be careful. I heard a great horned owl hooting just a bit ago. If'n you happen near his nest, he's apt to light out after you," she warned.

"I'll watch out, Mrs. Abbott. Good-bye," Josie said. As she started at a run across the field, she was careful where she stepped. With ten cows grazing, a lot of obstacles dotted the pasture.

"Whoo-whoo-whoo, who-whoo, to-whoo-ah" came a call from somewhere in the woods.

Despite her haste, Josie stopped. A great horned owl didn't have such an even-pitched hoot. That sounded more like a harmless barred owl. Not many people knew the difference, but Josie was sure she recognized the deep-toned cry. And, after all, why shouldn't she? These woods were like home to Josie.

Home. That's what she wanted right now.

Home, where her mother and brothers would welcome her. She longed for them to comfort her and tell her everything would be all right. As she headed for the woods, she deliberately blotted out the image of Uncle Hiram. He had no part in her homecoming.

Through the Woods

Though the weight of her bundle dug into Josie's shoulder and her arm ached, the closer she got to home, the faster she walked. Without even the glimmer of the moon or a star to guide her, she found her way past the barn and the smokehouse and through the gate that fenced in her mother's gardens from the livestock.

When Josie saw a glow of light from the kitchen window, she dropped her bundle on the porch and looked in the window. Susan Dexter, wearing the calico dress Josie had made for her, was in her rocking chair mending. Sam and Robert were seated on stools at the kitchen table playing checkers. With Uncle Hiram nowhere in sight, Josie pushed open the back door.

"Ma," she called quietly. In the shadowy light of the lard oil lamp, Susan Dexter looked tired. For the first time she seemed old to Josie. But when she glanced up and saw her daughter, her face brightened, and she looked the same as ever.

Sam and Robert jumped down from their stools. The three of them looked so good to Josie, their expressions so welcoming, she just stood in the doorway foolishly grinning. Though none of the Dexters had kissed since the day their father died, Josie suddenly wanted to throw her arms around her mother. But the family had never been affectionate with each other, and Josie thought her mother would be embarrassed. After all, she had just been home five days before.

"I'm pleased to see you, Ma," is all she said, but she hoped her mother heard the warmth behind the words. "And you too, Sam and Robert," she added. She couldn't help thinking how Will would have run to her with one of his bear hugs.

"Josie, I'm glad you're back," Susan Dexter said. She brushed off the threads from her lap and stood up. She glanced toward the hall as she hastily folded her mending and laid it on the chair. "I've been baking all day. Let's set on the back steps and talk where it's cool," she suggested.

"Yeah, then Uncle Hiram can't hear us. He's been drinking, and Ma told us not to vex him," Sam said more practically.

Josie tried to catch her mother's eye, but Susan Dexter's face was expressionless. "Hush

Sam, that ain't true," she said.

"It is too, Ma. Sam and me saw him out by the barn with his jug," Robert declared as he and Sam followed Josie and their mother onto the back porch.

Josie touched her mother's arm. "Did Uncle Hiram go to town today?" she asked.

Susan Dexter sat on the top step and nervously pushed the dark hair back from her face. Then she turned to Sam and Robert, who had settled on the bottom step with Josie. "I want you boys to check the barn. Toby's been snuffling 'round out there all night. Could be a fox. Shoo now," she ordered.

Reluctantly, the two boys started for the gate, slopping through the mud with their bare feet. Robert looked back reproachfully to show he knew they were getting rid of Sam and him so they could talk alone.

"See how pretty my dress is, and it fits just perfect." Susan Dexter ran her hands over her skirt.

Her mother hadn't answered her question. "Then Uncle Hiram did go to town today," Josie said flatly.

Susan Dexter stared toward the barn, where they could hear Toby's barking. Then she nodded. "Hiram was in a rage when he come home, Josie," she admitted. "And I gotta say, the stories he told me sounded peculiar. Something about you parading around a steamboat in soaking wet clothes, then picking up with some strange man? I didn't believe none of it."

"I did go on a steamboat trip, Ma, it's true. But the rest of the story got all twisted in the telling," Josie said as she began her explanation. She told her mother everything that had happened except the ending, that Mrs. Brown had dismissed her. If need be, that could come later.

When she was finished, her mother let out a long sigh. "I knew you wouldn't do anything bad, Josie. And folks telling tales about you and that man just ain't fair. Why, if it — "

"What just ain't fair?" Uncle Hiram's deep voice interrupted. Josie and her mother both jumped up. With the flickering lamp behind him, Hiram seemed to fill the doorway. He stepped onto the porch and peered into the gloom. "That ain't Josie out there, is it?" he demanded. Though he tried to speak each word clearly, his words were slurred.

Before her mother could answer, Josie spoke up. "Yes, it's me, Josie," she said, trying to pronounce each word carefully. "And . . . and what you heard in town today about me wasn't — "

"Susan!" Hiram roared at his wife. "I told

you not to 'low that girl in my house." He took another step forward, lurching on his bad leg. Instinctively, Josie cringed back, though she saw no stick in his hand.

"But she's my own daughter, Hiram, and after all, we ain't in the house, just on the porch," Susan Dexter spoke quietly, but Josie noticed how her fingers twisted in the folds of her skirt.

"The porch is as much a part of my house as the kitchen, and I want that girl gone from it," Uncle Hiram ordered.

"But Josie's my own daughter, Hiram, your brother's child — "

"Say no more, woman, I heard enough about her today to last a lifetime," Hiram interrupted. "She ain't welcome here ever again, in my house, in the barn, or anywheres. Do you understand that?"

"Josie's story ain't like what you heard," Susan Dexter objected. But her voice was faint and barely audible.

Josie was too dumbfounded to utter a word. As she followed the argument, she felt like a hoop being rolled from her mother to her uncle and back again. A whack from Uncle Hiram sent her in one direction, and a tap from her mother spun her in another. Out of the corner of her eye, she saw Sam and Robert walking toward the house with Toby following. When Toby realized it was Josie on the porch, he loped toward her, nuzzling his head in her skirts and barking. She tried to hush his racket with her hands.

Hiram had seen Sam and Robert too. "I ain't going to repeat it. I don't want Josie near my house or the boys." He jabbed the air in the direction of Sam and Robert, who had sidled around the herb garden to stand in the shadows of the house. "I want her gone. Now." Hiram's tone was final.

Oh, Ma, Josie begged silently, tell him this is your house, not his. And the boys are your sons, not his. Say it, she willed in a silent scream of protest.

Instead, Susan Dexter turned her wedding ring around and around on her finger. "Hiram's word is law, Josie," she said lightly as if it were a joke. But all of them knew she was serious. "You go on back to Mrs. Brown's for the night and we'll talk about it later."

Toby whined in pain as he tried to tug his head from Josie's grip. She hadn't realized how tightly she held him. "I'm sorry, Toby," she cried, leaning down and burying her face in his neck. Ma didn't stand up to Hiram, even when she knew I was right, Josie agonized as she squeezed her eyes tight with the hurt of it. She suddenly shivered. The night had blown in a clammy mist, and her skirts and feet were still damp. She would have to leave. But not like this.

"Walk a ways with me, Ma," she appealed to her mother as she picked up her bundle from the porch.

Susan Dexter looked at her husband with raised eyebrows as if to ask his approval. Without an answer, he turned on his heel and limped back into the kitchen, slamming the door behind him.

As soon as he was gone, the two boys ran out from the protection of the house, their eyes wide with alarm. "Josie, you got to stay," Robert cried. "You got to. You're our sister." Sam hung behind Robert. His face was stricken.

"Boys, I want you to go to bed right now," their mother ordered sternly. "All of you are taking this too serious. In the light of day, when your uncle feels better, he'll have forgot the whole thing. His temper's high now, that's all," she said more gently as she guided Sam and Robert toward the house.

Josie started slowly up the path. Her mother was probably right. Most of the time Uncle

Hiram didn't even remember what he had said or done in the morning after a drunk spell. But it didn't matter. Her mother had let her down. When Josie heard Susan Dexter's steps across the porch, she turned to wait for her. Her mother carried a tin lantern that lit her way.

"Ma, you know I didn't do anything wrong. Yet, you . . . you let Uncle Hiram send me from my own house and from you and the boys," Josie protested as they started up the path together. The lantern beamed a circle of yellow in the mist.

"There was nothing I could do, Josie. He's my husband," Susan Dexter said as if that explained everything.

"But I'm your daughter!" Josie almost shouted it out. "Don't I have any rights to see you and my brothers?"

Her mother looked down. "I guess not," she said simply. If the night hadn't been so still and her answer so clear, Josie wouldn't have believed she had heard it.

"He's beaten you. He's taken over Pa's farm and spent money on whiskey that should rightfully be yours. He's done nothing for you," Josie cried out her hurt.

A sudden slap on her face rocked her back on her feet. The shock of it jarred through her head. Susan Dexter lifted her hand as if to strike Josie again, then dropped her hand to her side. "He's my husband," she whispered. "Most times he's decent to me, and what am I without him? I got no place to go, no money, and no way to earn it. You know I can scarcely read and write. He'd even get to keep the boys. I'm nothing without him as my husband, don't you see?"

They had stopped walking and stood facing each other. The mist clung to the tall grass and smoked around their skirts. In the faint light of the lantern Josie could see the deep shadows in her mother's face. Susan Dexter always boasted she was born on the thirty-eighth anniversary of her country's founding, so Josie knew she was only thirty-four. She looked fifty.

All the anger drained out of Josie and left only pity. Her mother was right. She had nothing. She had even less than Josie. At least Josie had a strong back and a will to get along somehow. And she would get along. Never would Josie let herself be trapped like her mother, with no means to manage on her own if she had to. Or wanted to. Josie was filled with such compassion for her mother, she loved her as she never had before.

"Bye, Ma," Josie said softly. This time she leaned over and kissed her on her cheek.

Susan Dexter didn't seem embarrassed at all. She reached up and returned Josie's kiss. "Take the lantern to guide your way, Josie. And farewell. At least for now," she said. She handed Josie the lantern and turned to walk back to the house. Josie watched until her mother's slight figure was enveloped by the fog.

Now what should Josie do? Sneak back and sleep in the barn? Walk to Charlotte's? She was too tired. There was a stirring in the pasture. Their voices must have awakened the Dexter's cows. They made Josie think of Mrs. Abbott. That's where she would go. Mrs. Abbott needed help with the dairy. Maybe Josie could do that. It was at least worth a try, and even if Mrs. Abbott weren't able to pay her, it would be a place to live and be useful.

It wouldn't be like the mill, where no one even cared about her name. No, she would never return to the mill. And being at Mrs. Abbott's wouldn't be like working for Mrs. Brown, where talk about a person counted for more than what a person really was. Mrs. Abbott might have shortcomings, but paying mind to gossip wasn't one of them. Best of all, living so close, Josie could see her mother

and the boys from time to time.

With her bundle still over her shoulder, she opened the pasture gate to take the shortcut through the woods. She lifted her heavy skirts, and holding the lantern low to light her path, she picked her way across the muddy field.

"Whoo-whoo-whoo, who-whoo, to-whoo-ah." From the still darkness of the woods, Josie heard the call of the owl, and she hesitated. Yes, she was certain that was a barred owl's loud, clear hoot.

Josie remembered Mr. Nuttall's book and how he had described the different owls. But she already knew most of it from her own experience. In lots of ways, she knew as much about birds as any book, at least birds around this part of New York State. Perhaps someday she could be a naturalist like Mr. Nuttall. She headed for the woods. It was worth thinking about, and not any more farfetched than Charlotte wanting to be a typesetter. If she went to the convention tomorrow with Mrs. Abbott, maybe she would get an idea on how to start. If she wanted to go in new directions, the convention might be the best place to begin.

"Whoo-whoo-whoo, who-whoo, to-whoo-ah," came the deep cry, and this time a dark shadow glided from the woods. Josie held up her lantern as she watched the big bird swoop overhead on moth-silent wings. It was the silhouette of a barred owl. With a sense of satisfaction, Josie entered the woods. Now that she knew where she was going, she couldn't get there fast enough.

Epilogue

The nation's first Woman's Rights Convention was held in Seneca Fallls, New York, on July 19 and 20, 1848. About three hundred men and women turned out to hear the speakers plead for wider educational and work opportunities for women, changes in property and divorce laws, and full recognition for women in the courts. Elizabeth Cady Stanton presented the Declaration of Sentiments, a document copied from the Declaration of Independence, which listed eighteen grievances. It began, "We hold these truths to be self-evident: that all men and women are created equal; that they are endowed by their Creator with certain inalienable rights; that among those are life, liberty, and the pursuit of happiness. . . ."

During the convention, eleven resolutions were adopted. The ninth resolution, proposing that women be accorded the right to vote, was so startling some of the convention leaders had opposed including it in the program.

"The resolutions are of the kind called radical," reported one local newspaper. Other newspapers throughout the country took up the cry, ridiculing the ladies and their Declaration of Sentiments and Resolutions. But their ideas quickly took hold, and the convention became the opening gun in the battle for legal, social, political, and religious equality for women. As a token of the struggle, the mahogany center table on which the demands were written in Mrs. McClintock's front parlor on Sunday, July 16, 1848, is now in the possession of the Smithsonian Institution, Washington, D.C.

Of the sixty-eight women and thirty-two men who signed the Declaration of Sentiments at the convention, only one, Charlotte Woodward, lived to vote in 1920, the first national election in which women were allowed to cast their ballot. It had taken seventy-two years of hard work and disappointments for women to gain that basic legal right.

Josie Dexter and the other characters in *The Girl with Spunk* are fictional, with the exception of Charlotte Woodward and the five organizers of the convention, Elizabeth Cady Stanton, Lucretia Mott, Mary Ann McClintock, Jane Hunt, and Martha Wright. Josie Dexter, however, is typical of farm girls and working girls everywhere whose eyes were opened by the convention to a realization of how their lives could be improved and channeled toward new goals, not only legally and economically, but also in terms of human dignity and self-respect.